WAS IT A MIRACLE ...
OR WAS IT MURDER?

Sister Agnes was everything a young nun was supposed to be: innocent, angelically beautiful, and devoted only to God. Until she was accused of one of the most unspeakable crimes known to man.

The police say she's a murderer. Her mother superior says she's a saint. And now it's up to psychiatrist Dr. Martha Livingston to seek out the shattering truth hidden behind the silent convent walls ... and in the darkest corners of a fragile young girl's mind. ...

Agnes of God

See the Movie, Read the Book in SIGNET and MENTOR Editions

Agnes of God

A Novel by
Leonore Fleischer

BASED ON THE SCREENPLAY BY
John Pielmeier

WITH AN INTRODUCTION BY
Norman Jewison

A SIGNET BOOK

NEW AMERICAN LIBRARY

PUBLISHER'S NOTE

SIGNET, SIGNET CLASSIC, MENTOR, PLUME, MERIDIAN AND NAL BOOKS
are published by New American Library,
1633 Broadway, New York, New York 10019

First Printing, September, 1985

1 2 3 4 5 6 7 8 9

PRINTED IN THE UNITED STATES OF AMERICA

Introduction

In February of 1981 I was in Buffalo, New York, directing the film *Best Friends* when the curtain was going up on *Agnes of God* for the first time in Boston. Lee Remick, a friend of mine, was playing the psychiatrist, and I was asked to fly in for the occasion. I have followed this play since that day.

Raised as a strict Canadian Methodist, I have always been fascinated by religious subjects. I think most people, regardless of their religion, harbor a desire to believe or have faith in something outside of themselves. *Agnes of God* gave me the opportunity to make a film about the conflict between faith and logic. The world today seems to be in dire need of angels. It was this universal search for saints that first attracted me to the play.

An admirer of John Pielmeier's work, I consider him to be one of America's finest young writers. After obtaining backing from Columbia Pictures for the film version, I first met with Pielmeier in December 1983 to discuss ways to turn his stylized theatrical work into a movie. Translated into seven languages and performed in fourteen countries, the play was originally written for three actresses on a bare stage. The entire play took place in the psychiatrist's office, and with the exception of two chairs and an ashtray there was no set. As we began work on the screenplay, I had the idea of setting most of the story in a convent in Quebec, hoping to create an environment that would be unfamiliar and interesting to the audience. The atmosphere of French Canada, steeped in its Catholic history, provided a rich background for our story and allowed us to use both English and French dialogue.

I have found that adapting a play can be very tricky, since in the theater the playwright so often speaks to the audience through lengthy speeches or monologues. The dynamics change considerably with film. The best adaptations are usually the result of the director's being fortunate enough to work with the playwright and, using film language, introduce visual elements to help interpret much of the dialogue. With John, who is no stranger to the screenplay, I was able to retain the intensity of the interaction between the three women while expanding the landscape of the play and adding a number of supporting players who lent a needed quality of realism to the story.

Producer Patrick Palmer, my longtime collaborator, was able to obtain the services of the Academy Award–winning production designer Ken Adam, who, with the top-notch construction coordinator Richard Reseigne, transformed the historic Rockwood Academy Boys School in Ontario, Canada, into a convent in less than six weeks. With the incredible talent of cinematographer Sven Nykvist, best known for his work with Ingmar Bergman, the set was ready to be brought to life by the cast. Film editor Antony Gibb, who has collaborated with me on *Fiddler on the Roof, Jesus Christ Superstar, Rollerball,* and *F.I.S.T.,* had the artistic eye necessary to make this mixture of technicians and actors work on the screen.

The casting of Jane Fonda, Anne Bancroft, and Meg Tilly marks the first time I've made a film with women in all the leading roles. In that sense, I suppose this is my feminist film. It was a truly exciting experience to direct three of the most talented actresses working today.

Jane Fonda brought to the role of Dr. Martha Livingston the intelligence, intensity, and conviction that has placed her firmly at the forefront of her craft.

Anne Bancroft, chosen in part because she is strong enough to stand up to Jane in their many dramatic confrontations, lent a warm sense of humor to the role of Mother Miriam Ruth.

Meg Tilly brought a completely fresh approach to the role of Agnes. Raised on a farm in British Columbia, Meg has led a very simple life. Meg has a certain innocence, a naturalness, an honest and caring attitude often found in people brought up in the country.

With the help of this wonderful cast and my very talented crew, I hope that we have created a film that will make both believers and nonbelievers think about religion.

NORMAN JEWISON, DIRECTOR

Toronto
April 18, 1985

Prologue

It is dark, and the screaming is horrible to hear. It goes on and on, scream after scream, agony translated into sound waves. And there are moans now, low and fearful, mingling with the shrieks of anguish, more frightening than the screams. Then the moaning stops, and silence is the most terrifying sound of all.

I am afraid to see what lies beyond the door. Nevertheless, I use all my strength to force it open.

Christ, have mercy upon us! I have never seen so much blood in my life. . . . There is blood on the walls, on the bed, a pool of blood on the floor. . . .

And there, there under the bed . . .

One

It was more than an hour's drive, due west from the city. Although she was usually impatient behind the wheel, preferring to be somewhere rather than on her way, Dr. Martha Livingston was finding the journey all too short. Outside the windows of the BMW, the day was splendid, crisp and golden. The odd light peculiar to the shorter days of late October, slanting richly down through massed clouds that were black below and pink on their summits, bathed the landscape in the luminescence one finds in a Turner painting. But it wasn't the majesty of the landscape or the splendor of the autumn day that was the reason for Dr. Livingston's reluctance to end her drive. In fact, she was oblivious to the world outside the car windows. It was what awaited her when she reached her destination that troubled her.

At the thought of it, her brows creased in a frown, and her long fingers tightened on the steering wheel. Instinctively, she went for her cigarettes, driving with one hand while she rummaged in her large leather purse for the pack and lit one. But the cigarette, which usually could be relied on to calm her, was now having no effect at all on her anxieties. She had mixed feelings about this case, and almost all of them were bad.

As a court-appointed psychiatrist, Dr. Martha Livingston had already encountered most of the unpleasant aspects of the human condition. Strong, intelligent, courageous, she was accustomed to entering boldly the darkest hidden corners of the criminal mind. Her professional life dedicated to bringing the light of reason to bear on secret fears, she rooted out those fears, exposed them as irrational, and conquered them. But this case had aspects she'd never met with before, aspects which were, to say the very least, disturbing.

Murder was always horrifying, but the murder of a newborn infant was doubly so, not only in the deed itself, but in the insane waste of a new life. *Waste*. The word was ironic. The baby had been found in a wastepaper basket in the accused's room, strangled, the umbilical cord wrapped around its tiny neck.

Insane. That was to be Dr. Livingston's job at journey's end, to determine the sanity or insanity of the accused. If judged insane, the accused would not have to stand trial but would be remanded for life to an institution. Thoughts of the accused made Martha shiver, even though the car's interior was warm enough.

She hadn't wanted this case, she reminded herself for perhaps the hundredth time. She'd told them so, loud and clear, that day in the courthouse, after the suspect had been arraigned.

"Get somebody else, please."

Justice Leveau shook his head firmly. "Sorry, Martha," he told her in that mellow judicial voice of his. "It's you."

"What about Roger?" she protested. "He's free."

Eve LeClaire, the Crown attorney, broke in with brusque authority. "They want a woman," she said flatly, as though that put an end to all arguments.

She'd known all along it must be something like that, known it when the phone call had come, requesting her presence at the arraignment. She'd known it as she stepped over the cables trailed by the television news cameras and pushed her way through the crowd of excited reporters on the courthouse steps. There had been pandemonium on the broad marble staircase of the large courthouse, a hubbub of voices yelling and talking English and French. Ahead of her she had seen the accused, pale, small, and very thin, surrounded by the others and flanked by

Eugene Lyon, a defense attorney who always managed to latch on to the headline-making cases.

And this case—with all its bizarre elements—had made headlines. Not only here in Montreal, not only in the province of Quebec, not only in Canada, but around the world. This was sensational front-page stuff, and Martha Livingston wanted no part of it.

She looked around the richly paneled and book-lined room that was Justice Joseph Leveau's chambers. Her colleagues outnumbered her three to one. Leveau, LeClaire, and Lyon, comfortable and smug, sat around in their leather chairs, while she stood, all nerves, puffing desperately at her third cigarette in twenty minutes.

"All you have to do is meet with her once or twice," began Lyon with his best courtroom persuasiveness, "and then tell the court she's insane."

Martha wheeled on him, her dark blue eyes snapping furiously. "Are you dictating my position to me?" she demanded.

LeClaire interposed smoothly, "Martha, all we're saying is . . ."

But Dr. Livingston was not to be soothed. "We're getting into some sticky legal territory here," she insisted.

"Nobody wants this case to come to trial," the prosecuting attorney retorted. "Not the Church, not the Crown, least of all, me."

Martha ground her cigarette out savagely in the nearest ashtray and automatically reached for another. "Come on, Richard, she strangled a baby ..."

"Nobody's interested in sending a nun to prison," LeClaire insisted.

The judge shifted in his armchair, exhibiting the first sign of discomfort he'd shown thus far. "We're not telling you what to decide, Martha," he said, although the expression on his face meant just the opposite. "We're not even telling you to take this case. It's just that we're under a lot of pressure here."

"Is there any reason why you feel you shouldn't take it?" asked the defending attorney, Lyon.

"Yes," answered Martha immediately, and then bit her lip. How could she explain her objections when she couldn't completely articulate them to herself?

"What's that?" asked Lyon pleasantly, but his sharp lawyer's eyes probed her face.

What can I tell them to make them understand, Martha asked herself. I'm the wrong doctor for this case. Even more important, this is the wrong case for me.

"Today's my birthday," she said at last. "I always make bad decisions on my birthday." She knew her words were too flippant, too brittle, but there was such a tightness in her throat that these were the only words she could voice.

They laughed. Then the judge reached over and picked up the file folder containing the documents in the nun's case. With a small sardonic smile, he handed it over to Martha.

"Happy birthday."

Reluctantly, she took the folder. "Thanks." It felt light in her hand; there couldn't be too many documents in it. Why should there be? It was open-and-shut, right? A nun would have few documents to tie her to the bureaucracy of the outside world. And no priors. A prioress, maybe, but no priors. Martha winced at her own bad joke; it was a signal from her subconscious that she was getting tired and ought to be on her way while this masculine judicial trio still left her in one piece.

Tucking the file folder into her briefcase, she said her good-byes as graciously as she could, considering the way the three had steamrolled her. Her heels tapped too loudly in her own ears as she crossed the marble floors of the courthouse lobby; her nerves were raw. She hadn't taken step one on this case and already it bothered her.

A nun, she thought as she unlocked her car and threw her briefcase onto the backseat, as far away from her as possible. A nun and a murderess. No, not murder. She kept forgetting that the charge was manslaughter. A nun was indicted for manslaughter. Even so, Sister Agnes had killed her own newborn baby, strangling it with its umbilical cord. What a mess! Martha muttered to herself. No wonder this case has me turned off! Christ! A nun!

Dr. Livingston attempted to picture Sister Agnes as she drove home. She tried to recall the figure she had seen on the courthouse steps, a slight, small-boned figure surrounded protectively by a group of other nuns. Her face had been as pale as the white wimple she wore, but of her features, Martha could distinguish nothing. In the glare of the popping flashbulbs, details of the girl's features had been lost, though her eyes had left an impression. Large, the pupils were wide and dark.

She looked straight at me, Martha thought, and she was scared out of her mind.

Out of her mind. She must be, mustn't she? What other kind of mentality strangles a newborn? Was it premeditated or at least temporary insanity?

Whatever, Martha had already decided that the best thing to do was to make short work of this case, as Lyon had advised. Meet with Sister Agnes once or twice and turn in her diagnosis. What was the point of dragging this sordid mess out? The sooner it was over, the better for everybody concerned.

But now she tried to put it out of her mind. It was her birthday, she was going out tonight to celebrate it, and she would have just enough time to wash her hair and get dressed before her date picked her up.

But a nun! Jesus Christ! A nun!

"Bonne anniversaire, Marty," Richard Langevin whispered in her ear, under the cheerful din of restaurant noise. He gave her earlobe a little nip of affection, but Martha shook her head impatiently. The others at the table began boister-

ously singing "Happy Birthday to You" as the beaming maître d' brought the cake over, its icing festive with sparklers. Rive Gauche was her favorite restaurant, her birthday was her favorite time, the singing people her favorite friends, and Richard Langevin was dear to her, but Martha couldn't shake off the feeling of dread that had ruined this day. That damned case! She couldn't keep her mind from turning to it; not the rabbit pâté, the duckling with Normandy apple brandy, or the good Bordeaux could distract her. Not even this faintly ridiculous and embarrassing cake, which had everybody in the bistro now joining in the song and applauding.

A bottle of champagne arrived as if by magic, compliments of the house, and Martha made an effort to look as if she was enjoying herself. She had dressed with special care and the admiration on Richard's face told her she was looking well, her slim body outlined by the silky jersey of her best dress, her long neck and prominent collarbones showing to advantage. After all, this was a special occasion.

But whenever she closed her eyes she could imagine a baby, blue-faced, a bloody cord around its neck, its unseeing eyes popping from their sockets, its tiny hands clawing for merciful air, and she shuddered.

It was after midnight when they left the little bistro in Old Montreal. The three couples stood on the slick cobblestones—it had rained while they were in the restaurant—noisily saying good-bye. They were all tired from the long day and more than a little tipsy from the wine added to the champagne and the after-dinner cognac. Martha had a headache, which had wound itself tightly around her skull and made its ferocious way into the sockets of her eyes.

"You didn't have a very good time," said Richard ruefully as they climbed into his ancient Peugeot.

She reached over and squeezed his hand. "I did. Really. I'm sorry. It's this goddamned case they put me on today."

"The nun who killed the baby?"

She nodded wearily.

"*Dommage,*" he sympathized. "I don't envy you. It's not going to be an easy determination."

"Don't I know it!"

The streets were shiny with wet under the antique streetlights of the Old Quarter. They drove slowly and in silence, out of deference to Martha's headache, but Richard Langevin kept casting sidelong glances at her pale face, as though he were burning to ask her questions. As a lieutenant of detectives, he *was* burning to ask her questions. This case, with all its headline-snatching ugliness, seemed to him cut and dried. A nun had somehow borne an illegitimate baby secretly and had disposed of it by strangling it. But after that, it got political. Not only were the Crown authorities involved, but the leaders of the Roman Catholic Church in Canada were watching it very closely, ready to step in if they thought it necessary.

The Peugeot climbed into Mount Royal Park; Martha's apartment was in a converted Victorian mansion in the English-speaking Westmount section on the slopes of the park. At the summit of Mount Royal stood a tall lighted cross, visible from much of the city. Although it was a familiar landmark, Martha's eyes were drawn to it now, and she couldn't look away. The whiteness and purity of the symbol seemed to be burning into her aching brain. Her head was about to split from the pressure of its brightness.

They pulled up in front of her apartment building but made no move to get out. Richard was on duty later tonight. Even so, unspoken between them was the decision that tonight was not the right time for him to come up and stay. He fished his rumpled cigarette pack out of his pocket and lit two, handing one to Martha without a word. They sat smoking in silence for a minute, then Langevin spoke.

"This nun. What do you know about her?"

Martha shook her head in annoyance. "Will you stop playing detective, Richard? Leave your badge at the office. Okay?"

"Marty, there are important investigative questions to be asked here."

"Like what?"

"Like are they really bald underneath that headdress?" The question was so unexpectedly ridiculous that Martha couldn't stop a whoop of laughter.

"No, I'm serious," Langevin continued. "When

I was a kid, they told us nuns lived to be a hundred and fifty."

"Well, don't they?" Still a little tipsy from dinner, they giggled like a pair of naughty children.

Again, a silence, while Martha took a deep drag on her cigarette. "Richard, I don't know if I can take this case," she said quietly, now serious.

"Why not? Look, if you're worried about it, give it to Roger. Nothing bothers Roger—"

"Did you know I had a sister?" interrupted Martha suddenly.

Langevin turned to her, his keen dark detective's eyes under their craggy brows searching her face. "No," he said quietly, and waited to hear.

"Marie was a couple of years younger than me." The words came out with difficulty, as though they'd been kept hidden so long that they were afraid of the light. "She entered a convent when she was sixteen. She died there of acute and unattended appendicitis because her mother superior wouldn't send her to the hospital." Marty stubbed out her cigarette and stared straight ahead, not meeting Richard's eyes.

"Jesus," Langevin breathed. The bitterness, not only in her words but in the tone of her voice, was all too evident. Martha's anxiety and her reluctance to take this case were clear to him now. Nuns, convents were anathema to her. For years she had carried around with her this anger and this pain.

Now she turned to face him, and a small wry smile tugged at her full lips.

"So, you know, me and religion." She tapped her forehead. "This. This is my religion. Up here. It holds the answer to absolutely everything."

The oldest conflict in history, thought Langevin. Faith versus reason, reason versus faith. And she thinks she's got it knocked. Aloud, he said only, "Yeah, the answer to everything except whether or not you should take this case," and gave her a small kiss on that rational brow she was so proud of.

"I'll sleep on it." Martha laughed. She was feeling better now; Richard always had that effect on her. He was so solid, so dependable. He even looked solid, with his rugged face, large capable hands, warm eyes, and shoulders made of granite. She smiled fondly at him, wishing for the moment that she could ask him upstairs.

Langevin looked at his watch. "Jesus! I gotta be at the station in twenty minutes!" He started up the engine.

Martha climbed out of the car. "Thanks for the party, Larry, it was great! Don't bother walking me to the door."

"Happy Birthday. I'll call you." He drove very slowly ahead, keeping his eye on Martha. When she reached her doorway, he switched on the police spotlight that sat on top of his car, catching her full in its beam, lighting up her slim figure. She turned and waved goodnight to him, smiling.

The lift in her mood lasted until she reached her apartment. She let herself in with her key and reached for the light switch but changed her mind. The dark was somehow comforting, and she could see surprisingly well in it. She dropped her purse, keys, mail, and newspaper on the hall table that held her telephone answering machine and switched the machine to "Message Play," turning up the volume so she could hear it from the kitchen.

A small black-and-white cat came scampering toward her, meowing for attention, following Martha into the kitchen. Over its insistent demands for food, Dr. Livingston could hear her messages being replayed in the muted electronic echo of an answering machine.

"Hi, Marty, it's Helen." Her secretary, Helen Gervaise. "Just called to tell you that Mrs. Davenport phoned to confirm her appointment at nine A.M. tomorrow. Okay, bye-bye." Click.

Martha opened the refrigerator and took out a carton of milk.

"Hi, sweetie, it's me." Tom's voice. "Just wanted to wish you a happy birthday. Sorry I couldn't be there tonight. I'll call ya tomorrow. Love you." Click. Martha sighed and shook her head.

Pouring herself a glass of the milk, she took the cat's saucer out of the overhead cupboard. Mitzi purred and wound around her legs as she smelled the milk coming her way.

Martha stood in the open door of the refrigerator, sipping slowly at her milk by the light of the tiny bulb. At her feet, her cat lapped happily from its saucer. The next voice issuing eerily from the machine made her straighten and put the glass down carefully with trembling fingers. As usual, he spoke in both English and French, switching from one language to the other with natural ease.

"Hell, Martha, guess who?" Very funny, Martha thought. "I wanted to wish you *bonne anniversaire. Bien des choses à ta maman.* And give me a call sometime, okay? *À bientôt.*" Click.

Even though they'd been divorced for five years, the sound of her ex-husband's voice still rattled her. Jacques always phoned so unexpectedly, so casually, as if he were sure of his welcome. In her present fragile state of nerves, Martha was glad she'd missed the call. Yet a feeling of warmth suffused her; she was equally glad he'd called.

A last message. "Marty, it's Helen again. Mrs. Davenport just called and wants to cancel tomorrow completely. See you."

Click. Its duties fulfilled, the machine turned itself off.

There goes my last excuse. No appointments tomorrow. A full day in which to visit the convent and come face-to-face with the killer nun. Terrific.

Suddenly, Martha didn't want to be in the dark another moment. Shutting the refrigerator door, she snapped on the kitchen lights and walked back into the living room, switching on the lamps as she went. The cat, finished with her meal and now wanting a lap, trailed after her.

The mail that she'd thrown onto the hall table in the dark had mostly landed on the floor. Bending down to pick it up, Martha found the case folder Justice Leveau had given her also on the floor, its contents spilling out onto the carpet. Mechanically, she gathered the papers together, squaring their edges and putting them back into the folder. The folder itself she placed on the hall table, next to the evening *Gazette*, which she hadn't yet read.

NUN INDICTED FOR MANSLAUGHTER read the headline on the front-page story. Below the headline was a photograph of Sister Agnes. Although the photograph was rough and grainy, like all newspaper pictures, one could still see that the nun was young, very young. And quite pretty, even beautiful, with a smooth face, her eyes staring out, widened by terror. Young, pretty, and obviously very much afraid.

Dr. Livingston stared down at the photograph, which stared back up at her, as if pleading. Was this the face of a murderess? Sane or insane? She was about to find out.

Hello, Sister Agnes.

Suddenly, she was exhausted; it had been a long and emotionally loaded day. She laid the newspaper back on the table and walked slowly to the living-room window. The night was very clear, and much of the city was spread out to

Martha's view. Church spires like long stone fingers reached up to touch the stars. On the top of the mountain, above her head, the lighted cross seemed to challenge her, as though probing into her precious mind, testing to see what she was made of.

TWO

The road took a winding turn, and the flatness of the ground gave way to a gradual but pronounced rise. After the car had climbed for ten minutes or so, the road wound again into a turn. At the end of it, at the top of the rise, a high stone wall, iron gates, a looming set of gray buildings. The convent. She was there.

The convent and its surrounding walls were built of the same stone, quarried from the granite of the Canadian mountains and rough-hewn to appear very old. Built in the Middle Ages Gothic of the mother country's famous cloisters, the convent did, in fact, seem to have been standing here for at least five centuries, yet it was no more than one hundred fifty years old.

The gate was locked. Dr. Livingston parked on

the gravel driveway at right angles to the ten-foot-high stone wall and turned off the ignition. Getting out of the car, she looked around. Set apart from the countryside it overlooked, the convent grew like a medieval walled city out of its rural surroundings. Inside the gate, Martha could see a series of flower and vegetable gardens, most of them depleted now that summer was over but one or two still bearing late blooms and root vegetables. A nun in a rough working habit, her wimple pinned back to keep it from flopping in her face, was kneeling in front of one of the vegetable rows, her hands deep in the soil.

On the left-hand side of the imposing iron gate, attached to the stone of the wall, was a brass plate. It was engraved, LES PETITES SOEURS DE MARIE MAGDALEN. The Little Sisters of Mary Magdalene. Underneath the sign was a bell, which Dr. Livingston pushed. It must have sounded only inside the mother house, because the kneeling nun working in the garden didn't even turn her head.

It was very quiet here, calm and peaceful. A few birds that had not yet flown south for the winter made swooping circles in the sky high above. Swallows maybe. Martha took a deep breath of the crisp air and, as though her blackened lungs protested against the invasion of pure oxygen, reached into her pocket for her cigarette pack and lit one up.

A bulky nun came out of the front door and strode toward the gate, her large winglike French

wimple fluttering in the autumn wind like a
snowy kite. Sister Marguerite was a woman somewhere in her sixties, and her face was creased by
labor and by scowling, for her temper was not an
easy one. As one of only two "outside" sisters,
she had as part of her duties answering the bell
and locking and unlocking the gate, a sort of
menacing Saint Peter. Now, as she approached
Dr. Livingston, her scowl became a ferocious glare.

"Hello," began Martha pleasantly. "I'm Dr. Martha Livingston. I'm the court-appointed psychiatrist—" She broke off as the nun's glare deepened, noticing that the sister's rage appeared to
be focused on the lit cigarette she was holding.
Quickly, almost guiltily, she dropped it to the
gravel and stepped on it to put it out.

Now Sister Marguerite's anger transferred itself to the squashed stub profaning the driveway. If looks could kill! Martha kicked it into the
grass where its offending presence was no longer
visible. *If that doesn't work, I'll eat the damn
thing.*

Grudgingly, the glare lightened to a black scowl,
and the gate was reluctantly unlocked. Like a
chastened schoolgirl, Martha followed Sister Marguerite up the pathway and in through the heavy
convent door, which closed with a definitive bang
behind her. Without a word, the sister pointed a
finger at a door off the vast hallway, and Martha
entered it.

It appeared to be a reception room, furnished
not unpleasantly with old but comfortable chairs

and a small table or two. Yet just being in a convent was making Martha nervous enough. She kept remembering how her sister Marie had died for no good reason in a convent before the age of twenty. On the wall hung a heavy wooden crucifix, with a carved polychrome statue of the crucified Christ nailed to it, blood dripping from his wounds, oozing from the crown of thorns depicted on His brow. The expression of agony contorting the features of Jesus made Martha fumble around in her purse for her cigarettes, even though the lack of any ashtrays in the room was telling her something. As she took out the pack and her lighter, she could almost swear that the agony on the Christ's face deepened a shade.

"Dr. Livingston, I presume." There was a hint of merriment in the voice, as if it could not resist this feeble and all-too-familiar joke.

Martha turned. A tall woman in an immaculate habit, wearing a close-fitting wimple and scapular of dazzling white, was coming through the doorway with a quick, light step. Her right hand was outstretched in welcome, and she was laughing at her own joke as she approached.

"I'm Mother Miriam Ruth."

Awkwardly, Martha shifted her cigarette pack and lighter into her left hand so that she could clasp and shake the hand held out to her.

"How do you do? I'm—"

"You needn't call me Mother if you don't wish."

"Thank—"

But Mother Miriam Ruth had no intention of

letting Martha get a word in edgewise. "Most people find it uncomfortable," she continued, smiling.

"Well—"

"I'm afraid the word brings up tne most unpleasant connotations in this day and age." She had a strong, deep, and melodious voice, and obviously she was fond of the sound of it.

"Yes—"

"So you may call me Sister."

"Thank you," said Martha, surprised she was permitted to complete the phrase, but Mother Miriam Ruth had finished for a moment. She shut the door to the room.

"You must have tons of questions," she called pleasantly over her shoulder. "You can smoke if you want to. Just don't tell any of the sisters. They wouldn't understand. Especially Sister Marguerite. She'd scare the pants off the pope." Moving briskly to the window, she opened it wide enough to let the cigarette smoke out into the fresh air. Obligingly, Martha went over to the window to light up so the odor would be carried outside the room.

"Besides, I miss them," said Mother somewhat wistfully.

Dr. Livingston's eyebrows shot up. "You were a smoker?" she asked incredulously.

"Two packs a day."

"Well, I can beat that," Martha said with a trace of bitterness.

"Lucky Strikes." Mother laughed at the shocked

look on the doctor's face. Lucky Strikes were
heavy-duty lung pollution. "My sister used to
say," she continued, "that one of the few things
to believe in in this crazy world is the honesty of
unfiltered-cigarette smokers."

"You have a smart sister." Martha smiled.

"And you have questions," replied the mother
superior, sitting down and folding her habit
around her. "Fire away."

For a long moment, the two women looked at
each other appraisingly, as though sizing each
other up for the battle to come.

Mother Miriam Ruth saw a woman in her forties who had once been very pretty. Now pretti-
ness had turned into a handsome refinement of
bone structure, a striking expression combining
intensity and intelligence. Dr. Livingston was
tall, about five feet eight inches, and slender in a
strong, almost muscular way. Her thick hair was
light brown and contained streaks both of lighter
blond and gray. Her nose was small and thin, her
lips full and womanly, with prominent teeth.
But it was the eyes you looked at first. Under
arched brows like the wings of a moth were two
eyes of a deep, clear blue, fringed with heavy
lashes. The gaze was direct, even piercing, as
though there were no secrets behind them, and
as though they could penetrate your secrets in a
single glance.

Dr. Livingston was dressed in a simple and
businesslike suit, but it was cut and trailored in
a way that whispered *expensive*. Her long legs

were emphasized by the smoothness of her hose, and her feet were shod in a pair of costly pumps of Italian leather.

Martha saw a woman some fifteen or twenty years older than herself, a woman whose face was more worldly than one expected in a mother superior. There was nothing of translucent saintliness in her expression; instead, an earthy, almost animal magnetism. There were lines in her face, yet the face itself was somehow very youthful and very alive. Perhaps it was the mouth, which was wide, the lower lip full and of a startling red color. It was a juicy mouth, even a sensuous one, startling in a nun. The hair one could only guess at, because the wimple hugged the face tightly so that not a strand showed. But the eyebrows were thick, black, and shapely; it was likely that Mother Miriam Ruth's hair was thick and black as well, coarse in texture and crackling with health.

The mother superior's eyes were extraordinary, set far apart, large and very dark, almost a velvet black. They were eyes that had known both joy and suffering and had retained both. You could confide in those eyes, and they would not look surprised at anything you could tell them. Those eyes had heard it all before.

Dr. Livingston took a deep breath and squared her shoulders.

"Who knew about Agnes's pregnancy?" she fired away.

"No one."

"How did she hide it from the other nuns?"

"She undressed alone, she bathed alone."

"Is that normal?"

"Yes."

Like stichomythia in Greek tragedy, the dialogue moved swiftly between protagonist and antagonist without a wasted syllable.

"How did she hide it during the day?" asked Martha.

Mother Miriam Ruth took a fold of her loose, heavy habit in her forefingers and gave it a little shake. "She could have hidden a machine gun in here if she wanted."

"She had no physical examination during this time?"

The mother superior put her head to one side and regarded the doctor calmly. "We're examined once a year. Her pregnancy fell in between our doctor's visits."

"Who was the father?" demanded Martha.

"I haven't a clue," Mother responded quietly.

With a sharp movement of her wrist, Dr. Livingston flicked the cigarette through the open window and paced nervously into the center of the room. "What men had access to her?"

"None, so far as I know." A very faint, bitter smile hovered for an instant about the nun's lips. For surely there must have been a man, it said.

"Was there a priest?" Martha persisted.

Mother Miriam Ruth's brow creased. "Yes, but I don't see—"

Now it was Dr. Livingston's turn to interrupt. "What was his name?"

Mother laughed, a rich, resonant sound that filled the room. "Father Martineau," she said through her chuckles. "But I don't see him as a candidate."

"Could there have been anyone else?"

Mother Miriam Ruth's smile faded. "Obviously there was," she said quietly, her eyes suddenly hooded.

"And you didn't try to find out who!" I mustn't raise my voice, Marty told herself. Must hold on to what little objectivity I possess.

"Believe me," began the mother superior, holding up her hands, "I've done everything short of asking Agnes—"

"Why haven't you asked her?" demanded Martha hotly, all thoughts of objectivity and calmness out the same window as the cigarette.

Mother Miriam Ruth stood up with great dignity, smoothing her habit around her thin body. Looking Dr. Livingston square in the eye, she replied strongly, "She doesn't even remember the birth. Do you think she'd admit to the conception?"

Martha found herself wishing that she hadn't been quite so hasty in throwing that cigarette out the window. "Look," she said as reasonably as she could, "somebody gave her that baby. . . ."

"But that happened some ten months ago. I fail to see how the identity of that somebody has anything to do with this trial," said Mother Miriam Ruth calmly. It seemed that the mother superior had gained control of the interrogation.

"Why do you think that?" Dr. Livingston wanted to know.

"Don't ask me those questions, dear. I'm not the patient."

Almost desperate, Martha fought to regain control of the situation. "But I'm the doctor!" she retorted. "I'm the one who decides what is or is not important here!" She glared at Mother Miriam Ruth, and the nun glared back.

"Look, Doctor," the mother superior said rather stiffly, "I don't know how to say this politely, but I don't approve of you. Oh, not you, personally, but . . ."

"The science of psychiatry," snapped Dr. Livingston, finishing her sentence for her.

The white wimple nodded slightly, and the voice took on a note of genuine authority. "Yes. I want you to deal with Agnes as speedily and as easily as possible. She won't hold up under any sort of cross-examination."

A pang of something very like righteous indignation stabbed through Martha. "I'm not with the Inquisition," she pointed out.

"And I'm not from the Middle Ages," snapped the mother superior with surprising brusqueness. "I know what you are. I don't want that mind cut open."

In three or four long, swift strides she reached the door and threw it open. Sister Marguerite was just outside, looking flustered, as though

she'd been caught eavesdropping, which in fact
she had.

"Sister Marguerite," instructed Mother Miriam Ruth, "call Sister Anne down here and ask
her to show Dr. Livingston to Sister Agnes's new
room, please."

Without another word, Dr. Livingston marched
defiantly past the mother superior and out into
the hallway to wait for Sister Anne.

Sister Anne, the other "outside" nun, was very
different from Sister Marguerite. There was no
malice in her, only a surpassing timidity, and
she was terrified of and terrorized by Sister Marguerite. Anne was in her forties, very plain, her
face already crisscrossed with wrinkles of near-
sightedness and agony. She wore thick-lensed
glasses and suffered frequently from appalling
migraine headaches.

She had one now, and as she led the way in
silence, she kept her right hand pressed to her
brow, as if to keep the pain contained. Her silence was due as much to her excruciating headache as it was to her timidity and to the rule of
their order that forbade the sisters unnecessary
conversation.

As Martha followed Sister Anne up the stone
steps and along the echoing corridor, she was
struck anew by the quiet of the place. Not the
quiet of meditation and contemplation, but the
silence of emptiness. This large convent housed
very few nuns these days. It had been built in an

age when dedication to God and the call to a religious life was still very strong, especially among girls who were not destined to be married. Now, in 1984, troubled souls turned less frequently to God than they did to psychiatry, alcohol, drugs, sex, and other panaceas. Many of the convent's rooms had been sealed off to conserve energy in this decade of rising fuel prices.

Here and there a nun did appear. Sister Therese, a strong, stocky peasant woman in her sixties, was ferociously scrubbing the staircase, and glared at the two who dared to walk on her newly washed steps. A young, ugly pockmarked girl wearing a different habit and the veil of a novice, the only novice they had now, walked past them down the steps with a bucket of soapy water for Therese. This was Genevieve, who would in a matter of months take the veil and become Sister Genevieve, the first postulant to enter the convent this year. When the doctor greeted her, the girl blushed and ducked her head in a silent reply. She was shy of everybody except Mother Miriam Ruth, whom she worshiped.

Above them, from the third floor, Martha could hear the sound of a woman's voice singing a gloria in a voice of remarkable purity. The Latin words came drifting toward them, clear and passionate.

Gloria in excelsis Deo
Et in terra pax hominibus bonae voluntatis . . .

Martha's mind translated the song automatically, almost involuntarily. *Glory to God in the*

highest and on earth peace to men of goodwill ...
Whoever was singing had the voice of a Renaissance angel.

They had reached the third floor and the voice came to them more strongly now, singing God's praises.

> *Laudamus te*
> *Benedicimus te*
> *Adoramus te*
> *Glorificamus te ...*

Down the long corridor they went, with the angelic voice swelling before them. At last, Anne stopped before an open door, beckoned to Martha, and glided away, even the beads of the rosary that hung from her waist somehow silenced from rattling.

Martha came up to the doorway and looked inside.

Sister Agnes's new room was no different from what the doctor had expected. Clean white walls, a narrow hard bed, a small table that held a pitcher for water and basin for washing. A wooden chest to hide a few meager possessions, a change of wimple, habit, underwear. On the wall, a plain wooden crucifix with a simple figure of Jesus, unpainted.

The room, which faced west, was flooded with sunlight from the last dying rays of the afternoon. On the windowsill sat a young girl singing the praises of God, from a full throat, like a thrush. Sunlight illuminated her face, giving her the ethereal quality of a medieval painting. Sister Agnes.

As soon as she heard the doctor in the doorway, the young nun stopped singing and turned. Her face was the one in the newspaper photograph, the same purity, the same wide, frightened eyes. Their color was indistinguishable, so large were the pupils.

"Hello," said Sister Agnes, getting down from the windowsill.

"Hello. I'm Dr. Livingston. I've been asked to talk to you. May I?"

"Yes," said Agnes.

Three

Martha didn't come far into the room but stood instead just inside the door so that Sister Agnes would not feel intruded upon right away. The girl appeared to be no more than eighteen or nineteen years old; her skin was white and soft, and her eyes were glazed with a faraway look, as though she saw something that other people could not.

"You have a lovely voice," began Martha.

"No, I don't," Agnes answered.

"I just heard you."

The girl shook her head. "That wasn't me," she denied more firmly.

"Was it Sister Marguerite?" joked the doctor, but Sister Agnes did not laugh or even smile.

"You're very pretty, Agnes."

This time a small frown appeared between the pale smooth brows. "No, I'm not."

"Hasn't anyone ever told you that before?" asked Martha gently.

The girl's frown deepened. "I don't know."

"Then I'm telling you now. You're very pretty and you have a lovely voice."

"Let's talk about something else." Clearly, compliments about herself made Agnes uncomfortable.

This was a good opening, an offer to talk about "something else," and the psychiatrist accepted it. Slowly Martha closed the door to the room and turned back to the girl, who watched her expressionless, her eyes unreadable.

"What would you like to talk about?"

"I don't know."

"Anything," Martha said encouragingly. "First thing that comes to your mind." It was a standard psychiatric ploy, an invitation to free association by the patient.

Agnes turned her pale face up to the crucifix on the wall above her bed. "God," she said in a near-whisper. "But there's nothing to say about God."

Making her way slowly to the other window without taking her eyes off the young nun, Dr. Livingston sat down on the deep sill. Now she and Agnes were facing each other, sitting almost side by side on the two windowsills.

"Second thing that comes into your mind."

"Love," replied Agnes.

"Have you ever loved someone, Agnes?"

"God," the girl replied in all seriousness.

"I mean another human," prompted the doctor.

Agnes smiled for the first time, her face lit up from within. "Oh, yes," she breathed.

"Who?"

"Everyone." The smooth white face was exalted.

"But who in particular?" Martha pressed.

"Right now?" asked Sister Agnes.

"Yes."

"I love you."

Martha wasn't expecting this answer, and it threw her for a minute. She attempted to evoke the horrid mental image of the strangled baby with the blue face and protruding tongue that had haunted her before, but it was impossible to associate it with this smiling pretty girl and the angelic voice and unfathomable eyes. Agnes sat framed in the window like the Madonna in a Flemish religious painting.

"But have you ever loved a man? Other than Jesus Christ?"

"Oh, yes."

Now maybe they were getting somewhere. "Who?"

Agnes's face glowed. "Oh, there are so many!" she exclaimed.

Martha reached for the only name she knew. "Well, do you love Father Martineau?"

The name brought an added rosiness to the glow. "Oh, yes!"

"Do you think he loves you?"

"Oh, I know he does."

"He told you that?" asked the doctor sharply, her eyes probing on Sister Agnes's face.

"No," the girl replied slowly. "But when I look into his eyes I can see."

"You've been alone together?"

"Oh, yes."

Martha drew in her breath. "Often?"

"At least once a week." Agnes's smile was dazzling, ethereal with joy at the memory. Clearly she had strong feelings for Father Martineau. Were those feelings returned? Could the priest be the father of the nun's child? Mother Miriam Ruth had laughed at the psychiatrist's suspicions. But were they indeed so laughable?

Dr. Livingston smiled back at the girl, sharing her joy. "Did you like that? Seeing him every week?"

Sister Agnes clasped her white hands so tightly together that the knuckles stood out like ridges. "Oh, yes."

"Where did you meet?"

"In the confessional."

A deflated, hollow feeling invaded Martha's insides. She thought had been so close, but now the truth, whatever it was, seemed to be moving further away, out of her grasp. She drew another deep breath. "Do you ever meet with him outside the confessional?"

The smile vanished from the nun's face and she stood up, moving away from Dr. Livingston and from the window. The sun had almost set and the room was beginning to get darker, slowly but perceptibly. In the gloom, Sister Agnes's white face shone like the rising moon.

"You want me to talk about the baby, don't you?" she demanded.

"Would you like to talk about it?" asked Martha gently.

Against the black habit Agnes was wearing, her hands fluttered like a pair of agitated white moths. "I never saw any baby. I think they made it up."

"Why should they?" asked the psychiatrist reasonably.

Agnes turned her face away. "I don't know," she answered in a voice muffled by fear and by something else, something that Martha couldn't yet identify.

"Do you remember the night they said it came?"

"No. I was sick."

"How were you sick?"

"Something I ate."

"Did it hurt?" asked the doctor softly.

"Yes."

"Where?"

The young woman grew more agitated; her eyes burned in her face. Fluttering hands paused at her waist, hesitated, then indicated below. "Down there."

"What did you do?" asked Dr. Livingston as gently as she could.

"I went to my room."

"What happened there?"

"I got sicker," said Agnes shortly. She took a

couple of steps toward the door, as if her intention was to fling it wide open and run down the
corridor, away from the ordeal of these pummel-
ing questions.

"And then?"

"I fell asleep."

Martha's eyes widened in astonishment, "In
the middle of all that pain?"

"Yes."

How can I believe anything she says? Martha
asked herself. Does she really remember this as
her version of the truth, or is she genuinely am-
nesiac about what happened? Or is she a total
liar? Mother Superior said that she doesn't remember the birth; has Agnes managed to deceive
a woman as obviously intelligent as Mother Miriam Ruth?

"But where did the baby come from?" the
psychiatrist insisted in her gentlest voice.

By now, Sister Agnes had retreated to the darkest corner of the room, like a trapped and frightened animal. "What baby?"

"The baby they made up," prompted Martha.

"From their heads."

"Is that where they say it came from?"

"No, they say it came from the wastepaper
basket."

"Where did it come from before that?"

There was a pulse beat's hesitation, then Agnes spoke in a hoarse whisper. "From God."

But Dr. Livingston wasn't having any. "*After

God, *before* the wastepaper basket?" she demanded point-blank.

"I don't understand!" quavered Agnes.

"How are babies born?"

"Don't you know?" the nun shot back at her.

"Yes, I know, Agnes, but I want you to tell me."

As a tormented animal will attack when it's cornered, Sister Agnes exploded. "I don't know what you're talking about!" she shrieked. "You want to talk about the baby! Everybody wants to talk about the baby, but I never saw the baby, so I can't talk about the baby because I don't believe in the baby!" She was panting now, and her eyes were rolling wildly in her head. To the psychiatrist she appeared to be on the verge of genuine hysteria.

Dr. Livingston stood up and moved toward the young nun soothingly, trying to calm her. "Then let's talk about something else."

But Agnes was in no condition to calm down. Spurred on by fear and anger, the adrenaline was flowing through her veins.

"No!" She flung her words at her tormentor. "I'm tired of talking. I've been talking for weeks and nobody believes me when I tell them anything! Nobody listens to me!" Leaving her corner, the girl almost ran toward the door.

"Agnes, I'll listen." Martha hurried after her. "That's my job."

But, desperate to escape, Sister Agnes already had the door open and was out in the hall, run-

ning swiftly down the corridor. "I don't want to
have to answer any more questions!" she yelled
over her shoulder.

"How would you like to ask them?" called Dr.
Livingston after her.

Agnes stopped running and turned to face the
psychiatrist. "What do you mean?" she asked
cautiously.

Dr. Livingston spread her hands out, palms
up. "Just like that. You ask, I'll answer."

A hesitant smile touched the girl's face. She
looked like a child being offered unlimited access to some magical kingdom. "Anything?"

"Anything." Martha smiled back.

The ride back to Montreal was in total darkness, but it made no difference to Dr. Livingston.
She didn't even notice. Her thoughts were rac-
ing, and she had all she could do to keep some
part of her mind on the road as she sorted out
her impressions. Both Sister Agnes and the mother
superior had been so different from what she'd
expected, the one so otherworldly, the other so
worldly. From her first impression, was Agnes
insane? she kept asking herself. But she couldn't
decide on a definite answer. First, she had to
discover whether the girl was lying or telling a
kind of truth that only she understood. And was the
mother superior trying to protect the nun's innocence, or cover up the girl's guilt? Once again,
she couldn't come up with an answer.

All Martha had was a somewhat confusing set

of impressions, and the sure knowledge that Sister Agnes was no ordinary nun, and Mother Miriam Ruth no ordinary mother superior. And a second appointment, for the following day.

She was keeping her promise, to let Sister Agnes ask the questions for a change.

"What's your real name?" asked Agnes rather shyly.

"Martha Louise Livingston." Martha smiled.

It was another glorious October afternoon, warmer than yesterday. Dr. Livingston had arrived at the convent several hours earlier than she had the day before so that she could spend more time with Agnes. She was eager to wrap this case up and get back to her usual way of life and her private practice. Then, too, she felt uncomfortable hanging around convents and confronting the tortured face of Jesus every time she lit up a cigarette.

They were walking in a field belonging to the convent. The wheat had been scythed in late August and stacked in the fields to dry. At the end of September it had been harvested and was now safe in silos, while all the field had left to show for its efforts was some coarse brown stubble and an unemployed scarecrow, flapping in the stiff autumn wind.

Agnes walked happily through the stubble as though it was a meadow studded with fresh clover and daisies. Dr. Livingston followed a few paces behind, smoking, careful that sparks from her cigarette not be carried off by the gusting wind to ignite the dry stubble.

"Are you married?" Sister Agnes asked ingenuously.

"No."

"Would you like to be?"

"Not at the moment, no," replied Martha truthfully.

"Do you have children?"

Dr. Livingston shook her head. "No."

"Would you like some?" Agnes's enthusiastic questions were childlike in their simplicity. Was it an act or was she genuinely this simple? Martha could not yet make up her mind.

"I can't have them anymore."

"Why not?"

Martha hesitated. "Well . . . I've stopped menstruating," she admitted finally. Odd, how that admission causes pain. Why should it? It's a normal fact of life. Yet it hurts to say the words out loud. Part of it is the getting old, I suppose, but that's not all of it. She had the nagging feeling of having been robbed of something, something important that made her in some way complete.

But the pain-loaded words seemed to have no significance for Sister Agnes since she passed over them without comment. Instead, she asked, "Why do you smoke?"

"Does it bother you?" Martha asked.

Agnes held up a warning finger. "No questions," she reminded the psychiatrist of their agreement.

Dr. Livingston conceded the point with a smile. "Smoking is an obesession with me," she explained wryly. "I guess I'll stop smoking when I become obsessed with something else. Any more questions?"

"One," said Agnes. Nearby, the scarecrow twisted in the wind, flapping its arms and legs like some grotesque dancer.

"What's that?"

The girl turned to look seriously into the psychiatrist's face. In the strong sunlight, it was possible to see the color of her eyes, at least what color they were now, for their hue kept changing from pale gray to light blue to the color of slate.

"Where do *you* think babies come from?" asked Sister Agnes.

"From their mothers and fathers, of course. Before that? I don't know."

Agnes nodded, then told the doctor confidingly, "Well, I think they come from when an angel lights on their mother's chest and whispers into her ear. That makes good babies start to grow. Bad babies come from when a fallen angel squeezes in down there, and they grow and grow and grow until they come out down there. I don't know where good babies come out." She broke away and ran from the stubble to the grassy meadow beyond, her habit trailing in the wind like a ship's sail. She was shouting now, like a little girl, and her voice was caught by the wind and torn into scattered shreds of sound.

"And you can't tell the difference except that

bad babies cry a lot and make their fathers go
away and their mothers get very ill and die sometimes! Mummy wasn't very happy when *she* died,
and I think she went to hell. Because every time
I see her she looks like she just stepped out of a
hot shower!"

Agnes had reached a tall maple tree and stopped
running, out of breath. Her face was translucent,
eyes shining, ecstatic. Catching up with her, Dr.
Livingston was reminded of the derivation of the
word *ecstasy,* from the Greek for *out of place.*
Sister Agnes's feelings seemed to Martha totally
out of place in the nineteen-eighties, and her
innocence of the facts of life, if the nun were to
be believed, was close to impossible in this day
and age.

Agnes slid down the tree to lie upon her back
in the grass, looking up at the sunlight filtered
through the few leaves that remained on the
branches. "And I'm never sure if it's her or the
Lady who tells me things. They fight over me all
the time. The Lady I saw when I was ten." She
reached her fingers up toward the branches as if
to pluck the last leaves. "I was lying on the grass
looking at the sun, and the sun became a cloud
and the cloud became the Lady, and she told me
she would talk to me and then her feet began to
bleed and I saw there were holes in her hands
and in her side and I tried to catch the blood as
it fell from the sky, but I couldn't see anymore,
because my eyes hurt because there were big
spots in front of them. . . ."

The girl was totally caught up in her vision. Dr. Livingston had never before heard such a jumble of imagery, part religious hysteria, part Freudian symbolism, like the imagined wounds of Christ and "the fallen angel" who "squeezes in down there." Was this psycho-babble the real McCoy, or was Agnes a very clever faker? This case was much more difficult than she had anticipated. And yet the girl appears so sincere, and her eyes were so innocent.

"And she tells me things," continued Agnes, her face beatific, "like right now she's crying, 'Marie! Marie!' But I don't know what that means."

Marie! Startled, Martha gasped, and her breath caught in her throat. Agnes sat up, her eyes focused on something that Dr. Livingston could not see.

"And she uses me to sing. It's as if she's throwing a big hook through the air and it catches me under my ribs and tries to pull me up, but I can't move because Mummy is holding my feet. And all I can do is sing in her voice. It's the Lady's voice! God loves you!" She turned her face to Martha, and it was paler than ever. "God loves you," she said again softly.

"Do you know a Marie?" asked Martha through stiff lips.

"No," said Agnes simply. "Do you?"

"Why should I?" Even to myself, I sound defensive, Martha thought. What is happening to me?

"I don't know." Agnes rose to her knees, preparing to stand up.

"Do you hear these voices often?" the doctor asked.

But Sister Agnes, standing, was shaking grass and leaves from her habit. "I don't want to talk anymore," she stated in a normal voice. "All right?" And she started back in the direction of the convent. The interview was over.

Martha Livingston stubbed her cigarette out carefully on the ground, making certain that no sparks still smoldered. Then she policed the butt for insurance, tearing the paper open, letting the tobacco scatter to the winds, until no danger of fire remained. As she did this, she watched Sister Agnes walking through the fields, as calmly as though nothing had happened.

Four

Mother Miriam Ruth was waiting for Dr. Livingston in her office, with Sister Marguerite in attendance. The mother superior greeted Martha in a friendly way, coming from behind her cluttered desk to shake the psychiatrist's hand.

"Well, what do you think?" she asked with a shrewd look and a one-sided smile. "Is she totally bananas or merely slightly off-center? Or maybe she's perfectly sane and just a very good liar?"

"What's your opinion?" countered Martha.

The nun thought for a moment. "Well . . . I believe that she's . . . not crazy. Nor is she lying."

Terrific, thought Martha. What does that leave us with, the Virgin birth? Next she'll be telling me that three wise men came out of the east on camels. Aloud, she asked, "But how could she have a child and know nothing of sex and birth?"

"Because she's an innocent," said the mother superior earnestly. "She's a slate that hasn't been touched except by God."

The old *tabula rasa* bit. "That's nonsense," snorted the doctor.

Instantly, Sister Marguerite crossed herself furiously, but Mother Miriam Ruth didn't turn a wimpled hair. Instead, her voice grew softer, and the expression in her huge dark eyes became more bland.

"In her case, it isn't nonsense. Her mother kept her home almost all the time. She's had very little schooling. When her mother died, Agnes came to us."

"She's never been out there, Doctor," concurred Sister Marguerite. "She's never seen a television show or a movie. She's never read a book."

"But if she's so innocent, how could she murder a child?"

"She didn't!" cried Mother Miriam Ruth. "This is manslaughter, not murder!"

She closed her eyes; the color drained from her face as she relived that night in her mind. Her voice, when she told her ghastly story, was ragged, and the mother superior drew her breath in with difficulty, as though every word was being dragged from her memory under torture.

Martha listened, half in fascination, half in horror. So vivid was the telling that she broke in only rarely with a question.

"It was dark, and we had already gone to bed when the screaming began. It was horrible to hear. It went on and on, scream after scream, anguish translated into sound waves. I didn't know where it was coming from. I grabbed up a lamp and went running down the corridor, holding the lamp high in front of me. The kerosene was splashing perilously but I couldn't pay any attention to it, even though there was the danger of fire, because the screams of pain came tearing at my brain. Behind me, I could hear Sister Marguerite running, too. The other nuns were gathered in the corridor, frightened, confused. They called out to me in French as I ran past them.

" 'What is it? What's the matter? Who is screaming? Mother, please tell us who is screaming. Mère, je vous en prie!'

"I barely saw the novice, Sister Genevieve, cowering against the corridor wall, her veil awry. She was so slow to move that I came close to knocking her down in my haste, but instead I pushed her aside. Around me I could hear Latin, the beseeching words of prayers. Sister Elisabette and Sister Geraldine, the one nearly blind, the other nearly deaf, were on their knees with their rosaries in their hands. They're both in their seventies, and were nearly drooling with terror, their lips trembling as they recited the paternosters. Nobody except Sister Marguerite is of any use in an emergency, and I thank God for her, evil temper and all.

"The corridor seemed to be a mile long, but

the screaming was nearer and nearer and at last
we reached the door. Agnes's room. I knew it
would be. There were moans now, low and fearful, mixed in with the shrieks of anguish, and
for some strange reason I found them more terrifying even than the screams. Then the moans
stopped, and that was the most terrifying of all. I
grabbed the door handle and turned it.

"It wouldn't open."

"Was it locked?" asked Martha.

"There are locks on all the sisters' rooms, but
they are never used, because only the mother
superior is allowed to have the keys. There was
no way that Agnes could lock herself in, but still
the door wouldn't budge. Something heavy had
been shoved against it, blocking it to hold it shut.
I kept pushing my weight against it, but I'm thin
and not as strong as I was when I was younger.
Again and again I pushed, until, mercifully, it
yielded a little, enough for me to squeeze through
the doorway. Sister Marguerite, who is heavy,
had trouble getting in the doorway, but I couldn't
stop to help her. It was Sister Agnes who needed
me.

"Christ have mercy upon us! I thought to myself. Agnes was lying on the floor, so white and
still. There was blood on her habit, blood on the
walls, on the bed, a pool of blood on the floor
beside the bed. I had never seen so much blood
in my life and I couldn't believe it had all come
out of one person, one small nun.

"I was afraid she was dead, because she didn't

move, but she was still alive. Her breath was very faint, but the bloody habit moved ever so slightly over her chest.

"I wondered how long it would take for an ambulance to come and knew it was long enough for a soul to be prayed out of purgatory.

"By the time the intern began cutting Agnes's habit off her body, she had lost consciousness again. With every stroke of his knife, Sister Madeline Marie shrieked as though the blade were cutting into flesh, not cloth."

"And then?" put in Martha breathlessly.

"At last they had all gone, the ambulance with its flashing lights and wailing siren, and a thin, pale girl strapped to a stretcher, more dead than alive. Now I must do what I must.

"They were still in the corridor, my handful of nuns, crying and praying and asking each other questions for which there are no answers. I went into Agnes's room alone, but Sister Marguerite watched me from the doorway.

"I was afraid of what I was going to see.

"I held my lamp high, and looked around the room. There was something under the bed. I had to stoop to pull it out, because it was so heavy. It was a wastebasket, heavy with the bloodstained sheets from the bed."

"And something more," Martha added.

"Something . . . at the bottom of the basket . . . under the sheets. Something soft and wet with blood. I touched it, and cried out without hearing my own voice. It was cold. My hands were covered with blood, but I made the sign of the cross over the little dead body, and I whispered the words of baptism."

"She killed it?" whispered Martha half to herself.

"This is manslaughter, not murder!" cried Mother Miriam Ruth.

"She'd lost a lot of blood, and she'd passed out by the time we found her," added Sister Marguerite.

"So someone else could have done it," said Dr. Livingston thoughtfully.

The mother superior's dark eyes widened in surprise. "No, not in the eyes of the police," she said slowly.

"But in your eyes?"

"We've told you what we believe," Sister Marguerite answered with some asperity.

"That she was unconscious, yes. So someone easily could have come into the room and done it," Martha said again.

Sister Marguerite gasped. "You don't honestly think something like that happened?"

The psychiatrist turned to Mother Miriam Ruth, who hadn't said anything. "It's possible, isn't it?"

"Who?" the mother superior demanded.

"One of the nuns," suggested Martha. "She found out about the baby and wanted to avoid a scandal."

"That's absurd," the mother superior burst out.

"No one knew about Agnes's pregnancy!" barked Sister Marguerite. "No one! Not even Agnes."

This was getting them nowhere, thought Martha. They kept going around and around in circles, unable to get away from the mother superior's claim that Sister Agnes was a total innocent for whom neither the birth nor death of the baby held any reality. And the psychiatrist was expected to swallow this theory whole, without gagging, and hand in her official opinion that the little nun was not fit to stand trial. It was maddening. She drew deeply on her cigarette and looked around for an ashtray. Of course there wasn't one, what was she thinking of? This was a convent, not a café. She flicked her ashes into the small wire wastebasket that stood next to the wall by Mother Superior's desk. God, how she wished that this case was behind her!

The day was still fair and the sun yet high as Dr. Livingston drove away from the Convent of the Little Sisters of Mary Magdalene. Martha's mood was one of total frustration.

There were elements in this case that just didn't fit. Not merely the intangibles of Agnes's mysticism, but hard facts that were simply missing. Whether Agnes believed it or not, she had given birth to a real flesh-and-blood baby, and that meant that somewhere there must be a real

flesh-and-blood father. Even granting her innocence on all matters sexual, how did she meet up
with this man? If she couldn't get out to him,
and he couldn't get in to her, which Mother
Miriam Ruth swore was the fact, then where in
God's name did the baby come from? It wasn't
found under a cabbage leaf, and the stork sure
as hell didn't bring it. And how could Martha
believe that the mother superior, worldly as
she appeared to be, even sophisticated, never
found out until it was too late that her little
mystic had a bun in the oven? No, things just
didn't fit.

Damn it, I'm a psychiatrist, not a detective,
Martha thought. It's not my business to unravel
this case, only the mind of the accused. Even so,
I've got a few questions for this Father Martineau. He was the only man with regular access
to the nuns, not to mention that Sister Agnes's
face lights up like a flare when she hears his
name. What time is it? Not yet two. What the
hell, I've got some time, so why not?

Spinning the wheel hard to the left, Dr. Livingston threw the BMW into an illegal U-turn
and headed back south, turning off the convent
road about a mile before the Little Sisters' driveway, making for the village of Berthierville
instead.

A small village in the heart of the Quebec
countryside, Berthierville always reminded trav-
elers of the hamlets of France. This town, too,

was built of native stone, with cobbled streets
and small irregular plazas, one of them boasting
a well with a pump. Even many of the trees were
the same—larches, lindens and poplars in addition to the ubiquitous Canadian maple trees. It
was like stepping back into the previous century
and seeing the old houses with bicycles parked
by the front steps. The only concessions to the
nineteen-eighties were the occasional pickup truck
and a television antenna on the roof of every
house.

As usual, the Catholic church was the town's
most prominent landmark, and the small rectory
where the priest lived stood next door. Martha
braked the car to a stop and turned off the engine. Walking up the short path to the front door,
she remembered to put out her cigarette, crush-
ing the butt into the stones of the pathway with
her heel.

There was a bell, and Martha rang it hard,
flinching slightly at its loud, harsh jangle.

The door was opened by a middle-aged woman
in a rumpled apron, her hair in curlers, a cigarette dangling from the corner of her lips.

"Oui?" she asked suspiciously.

"Le père Martineau, est-il chez lui?" asked
Martha.

"Pourquoi?" demanded the housekeeper with
a who-wants-to-know belligerency. It was obvious
that she had taken a dislike to the psychiatrist
on sight, unless she was this hostile to everybody.

"Je suis ici sur l'avis de Mère Miriam Ruth du couvent," lied Martha. Mother Miriam Ruth would probably take a fit if she knew that Dr. Livingston was snooping around here asking questions.

The mother superior's name was the magic word that caused the door to open. The housekeeper stood aside with very ill grace and allowed the English interloper into her kitchen. But she managed to have the last word.

"Wipe your feet," she snarled in English.

The kitchen of the rectory was warm, too warm. Even on this beautiful day a fire in the woodstove was going full blast. The old pine table was battered but scoured to an immaculate whiteness. Four mismatched chairs stood around it, their hard seats softened by little cushions worked in colorful cross-stitch. From a hook on the wall hung a collection of rosaries. Across from it, on the far wall, was the inevitable crucifix, of plain wood, simply carved with the Christ figure. Hanging next to it, a photograph of the pope arriving in Canada, obviously cut from the Sunday supplement of the local newspaper; a religious chromo of Saint Therese of Lisieux, and two calendars. One calendar was from the Quercy Funeral Home of Berthierville and contained all the Catholic days of feast and fast clearly marked in red. The other was from the Ford dealership and showed a bosomy blond girl lolling on the beach in the skimpiest of bikinis.

Martha turned at the sound of heavy feet clump-

ing toward the kitchen, and in walked Father
Martineau.

She could see immediately why Mother Miriam Ruth had laughed so hard at Martha's suspicions. Father Martineau had at least eighty
years behind him. He had hardly a tooth in
his head, and his ancient gnarled hands were
shaking as he clutched his cane. He could barely
stand upright. A shawl was wrapped tightly around
his shoulders and Martha understood suddenly
why the heat was on full blast in the stove. It
was to warm his ancient bones. A wealthier or
more fashionable community would have retired
the old priest twenty years before, but in Berthierville he was a beloved fixture.

As he greeted her with a smile, Martha also
understood why Sister Agnes had lit up at the
sound of his name. His smile was as sweet and as
innocent as a baby's, and just as toothless. In a
face as wrinkled as a tortoise's, his wise old eyes
shone with youth and goodness. One felt instinctively that he would understand; no matter how
horrifying the confession or stringent the pen-
ance, absolution was guaranteed.

The case of Sister Agnes was, of course, upper-
most in his mind. He had been praying for her,
for all the nuns, in their time of dreadful need.
Praying, too, for the soul of the dead child, whose
innocence had been desecrated by slaughter, as
in the days of Herod. And, of course, he would
be happy to tell her everything he knew, al-

though that, alas, was little enough. But first, the doctor must have a cup of coffee with him.

They sat at the scrubbed pine table. The coffee was black and had chicory in it, like the old country, and was served in bowl-shaped cups without handles, the same way they served it in France. From a cupboard, the priest produced a bottle of fine Irish whiskey and poured some into each of their cups. To keep his warm, he said, although it must have been seventy-five degrees in that kitchen.

"Les Petites Soeurs," he began in a voice surprisingly young, "they rise at five in the morning and are in bed by nine at night. They work all day long and take their rest only at prayers. They farm, you know. Oh, not on a grand scale, nothing like that, but they grow their own vegetables and even a little grain besides. They have one or two animals as well. For eggs and milk and cheese, because they themselves don't eat any meat. Actually, they eat very little of anything. They have some fruit trees and bushes, excellent fruit, by the way. Plums and pears and several different kinds of berries. They even run a little fruit-jelly business. Everybody works to put up the jars of jelly, and Sister Jeannine is in charge of the books."

"Do they get visitors in to buy the jellies? Male visitors?" Dr. Livingston wanted to know.

"No, no, they are a cloistered order, and receive no visitors. What few jars they sell are sold through the mail, with ads placed in the parish magazines. The Convent of the Little Sisters is totally devoted to meditation, fasting, and prayer. Even if a man could get to them, they would probably be praying. So the question is not only how he got in, but when."

"And you're the only man to see them?"

"I promise you, Doctor, even if I had the inclination, how could I possibly catch her? She would have to be a very slow and patient nun." The old man's eyes twinkled with mischievous glee.

Martha laughed so hard at the thought of the arthritic priest hobbling lecherously after the light-footed Agnes that she choked on her coffee.

"It would take me too long to even remember the mechanics." Father Martineau chuckled. Not that I ever *knew* them, of course." The two of them shared a quiet laugh, which was a relief to Dr. Livingston after the stresses of the past couple of days. "No," continued the priest, "they are a very rare and special people, these sisters. Only a few left, consecrated to the praise of God."

They sat for a moment in silence, and then Martha said, somewhat tentatively, "You were Sister Agnes's confessor, weren't you?"

The laughter faded from the old priest's face, and he turned a serious eye on the psychiatrist. "The secrets of the confessional are sacred," he reminded her.

"I know that, but we have a great deal at stake here. If I judge Sister Agnes to be sane, she's going to have to stand trial. If she's found guilty she may have to go to prison for a long time. And unless I have adequate psychiatric proof of her insanity, a sane judgment is what I'm going to have to bring in. And soon. I'm not asking you to tell me what she confessed to you. But I am asking you to tell me honestly whether you think she is as great an innocent as Mother Miriam Ruth believes her to be. I've seen evidence of this . . . mysticism . . . of hers, but I'm not ready to say whether it's genuine or not. Even if it is genuine, can it be defined as crazy? I confess I'm not so expert in that area." She laughed ruefully.

For a long minute, the old priest regarded her seriously, thinking over the doctor's words. Then he spoke slowly, and his voice was less youthful than before.

"These matters of faith are very complicated, even when they aren't concerned with manslaughter. On Agnes's sanity I'm not qualified to give an opinion, and even her soul, which she has shown to me, I feel inadequate to judge. 'Ou krineis, me krinesthe,' the ancient Greeks say. 'Judge not, lest ye be judged.' All I can tell you is that her faith in God is very strong, and she knows almost nothing about the ways of man."

"That's what the reverend mother says," answered Martha.

"If anybody knows Agnes's heart, it's Mother Miriam Ruth," said the priest simply.

"But there's got to be more to it than that, or there wouldn't be a dead baby or an arrest or a court-appointed psychiatrist like me."

Father Martineau sighed deeply, looking suddenly even older than his years. "I don't envy you this task, my child." He took Martha's hand into his crippled fingers. "Such responsibilities lie heavy upon the soul, to say yea or nay. It is power in its purest form, the power over the life of another. It is a power rightfully reserved only to God. Do you pray?"

Dr. Livingston shook her head. "No, Father. Not anymore."

"Then you rely only upon your own strength and intelligence?"

"Yes, I guess I do ... Yes," she added more firmly.

"Then I will pray they do not fail you."

She opened her mouth to say, "Please don't bother." Oddly enough, what came out was "Thank you, Père Martineau."

Five

The road to the convent was by now familiar terrain; Dr. Livingston no longer had to watch for the signs marking the turnoff. She hoped that this visit would be her last, but something in the deepest part of her mind assured her that it wouldn't. Wasn't she getting too involved in this case? After all, it wasn't up to her to decide guilt or innocence; that was up to the courts. It was for her to say only whether the nun was mentally fit to stand trial. Some *only*, she scoffed to herself.

She was getting to be as familiar a sight to the convent as it was to her. This time it was Sister Anne, not Sister Marguerite, who unlocked the great iron gate, carrying a capacious wicker basket over her arm. Sister came very close to smiling a welcome. Or maybe Martha was imagining it.

"Before we go inside," said the psychiatrist, "I'd very much like to see something of the convent grounds. May I?"

Sister Anne nodded, and her white wimple fluttered like doves' wings. "I must gather the eggs now. Perhaps you'd care to come with me, and I'll show you some of our outbuildings."

"Thank you."

The two women skirted the outside of the main house, taking a small worn path through the kitchen gardens to the back of the convent. There was a large barn of weathered wood, in which one lonely cow was munching hay from a manger that could have accommodated a herd of thirty or more. Across from the barn stood a stable and a small chicken house; a few chickens were scratching in the dirt outside, muttering to themselves.

The chicken house smelled so awful that Martha wished that she dared to light up a cigarette to fill her nostrils with smoke. Sister Anne didn't seem to notice the smell as she felt around in the nests, lifting eggs out carefully and placing them gently into her basket.

"It's a large place," remarked Dr. Livingston.

"This convent was built for over fifty. There are fourteen of us now. We used to make our own bread, cheese, preserves, and sell them for income. Now all we manage are some jellies at Christmas."

"How do you survive?"

"We own the land around here and rent it out," replied the nun in a strong French accent. "We keep a few acres for ourselves; some corn, wheat, some vegetables."

"You work the land alone?" asked Martha curiously.

Anne shot her a look. "Yes, of course, with God's help. Sister Luke and Sister Mary Joseph do much of the heavy gardening because they are best suited to it. But all of us except the very old and the very ill work on the land. No one but Sister Marguerite and I are permitted any contact with the public."

Dr. Livingston gazed across the farmyard to the stone bulk of the convent. "Which was Sister Agnes's old room?"

At the mention of Sister Agnes, Sister Anne straightened and pressed her fingers hard against her brow; she could feel a headache beginning somewhere at the base of her eye sockets. Without a word, she pointed to a room high up, above the other nuns' third-floor bedrooms.

Why was Agnes kept separated from the others?

When Martha asked to see the room where Agnes had given birth, Mother Miriam Ruth's eyebrows shot up, but after a second she merely nodded.

"I'll take you there myself."

The mother superior was strangely quiet as they climbed the steps, but Martha could sense her disapproval. The psychiatrist was probing more deeply than either woman at the outset had expected she would. What was there to learn from an empty room?

And empty it was, and locked. The mother superior selected a long iron key from the bunch she was carrying and inserted it into the lock. It turned easily, and the door swung open.

A smaller room than Agnes had now, it was nevertheless very bright, with an almost unrelenting wash of pure white sunlight flooding it. There was no furniture in it at all, except a narrow wooden bed, stripped of its mattress. Even the crucifix was gone; only the shadow on the wall remained where it had hung, as though God Himself had departed, leaving only memories behind.

The floors and the walls bore evidence of recent, hard scrubbing which, of course, cleaned away the blood, Martha realized. Nothing else remained. Whatever mystery had been in this room was still locked inside Sister Agnes.

Dr. Livingston could almost hear Mother Miriam Ruth saying, "Satisfied?" in a dry voice. But instead, all the nun said was, "This place is locked solid. Ten-foot-high stone walls, one heavy iron gate, and Sister Marguerite's the only one with a key and she wouldn't let Christ in after dark."

"It's been known to happen in the day, too. Maybe Agnes went to him."

The mother superior shook her head impatiently. "Oh, come on! You've talked to her. She doesn't even know how babies are born, let alone made."

Surrounded by emptiness, the two women confronted each other, face-to-face, blue eyes locked onto brown.

"When did you first learn about her innocence, about the way she thinks?" asked Martha.

"A short while after she came to us."

"And you weren't shocked?"

Mother Miriam Ruth smiled her one-sided smile. "I was appalled. Just as you are now."

"What happened?" asked the doctor.

The smile faded from the mother superior's face. "She stopped eating. Completely."

"This was before her pregnancy?"

"Almost two years before."

"Why?" Martha prodded.

"She said she'd been commanded by God . . . I remember seeing her face only dimly revealed in the light of the chapel candles. Her eyes were enormous staring at me, her thin body trembled. It was quite plain to me that she was frightened of something. But of what?

"In the last week I had noticed suddenly how skinny she was getting, although Agnes was always too thin. But this was different. There were shadows under her eyes and hollows in her cheeks. Her habit hung from her shoulders like rags on a scarecrow. Even though her body didn't show through the thick folds of cloth, you could tell by just looking at her that her ribs must be sticking out. When I asked her if anything was wrong, she avoided my eyes when she said, 'No, Reverend Mother.'

"So I watched her. Mealtimes at the convent are a sacred time, a kind of Christian communion. The sisters do not speak; they pass the bowls and plates and ask for things by nods of the head and pointing fingers. I sit at the head of the table, and I read the daily offices out loud. Apart from Sister Susanna, who works in the kitchen, bakes the bread, and tastes everything, the sisters eat very moderately. If you don't count the communion wine, we drink only water.

"But Agnes was eating nothing. I kept one eye on her even as I read from my breviary. She would pass the bowls of vegetables and bread and take nothing at all for herself. The other sisters noticed this, but none of them had said anything to me. Sometimes I think they are all jealous of her, suspecting me of playing favorites."

"And are they right?" Martha asked with an ironic smile.

But Mother Miriam Ruth only raised one black eyebrow and continued her narrative.

"After every meal, Agnes would rise to clear the table, putting her own plate on the bottom of the stack, in order that my attention not be called to it. I said nothing in front of the others.

"But after a few days of watching her, I knew I had to speak. So when I found her kneeling alone in the chapel, in the near-darkness, I seized my opportunity and knelt down beside her, cornering her pretty effectively.

" 'You do not eat.' I started.

" 'No, Reverend Mother.' Agnes replied in a voice so low, it was almost a whisper. I leaned forward to hear her and whispered, too.

" 'Why not, Sister Agnes?' I asked.

" 'God has commanded me not to,' Agnes replied.

" 'He spoke to you Himself?'

" 'No.'

" 'Through someone else?'

" 'Yes.'

" 'Who?' "

Martha leaned forward, her face alight with eagerness.

" 'I can't say,' Agnes told me, and she looked away so that I could not see her eyes. She was huddled under her heavy habit for protection, and—and this was odd, because in the chapel the nuns hold their rosaries in plain sight so they can tell the beads while they're praying—Agnes's hands were hidden in the folds of her robe, under her scapular, as though they were freezing. It was cold in the chapel. Even the light of the candles was cold, pale and white, like frost. Like Agnes's forehead.

" 'Why?' I asked her because I felt I had to get to the bottom of this. For one thing, it was my responsibility as mother superior. For another . . . well, never mind. But Agnes is different from the others.

" 'She'd punish me.' Agnes told me.

" 'One of the sisters?' I asked her.

" 'No.'

" 'Who?'

"Just then there was a noise from the back of the chapel, and Sister Agnes jumped as though she had been struck. I had never seen anybody so nervous before.

"The noise was only Sister Paul, who is dead now, may God rest her soul. She was close to ninety then and was struggling to her feet, stiff with rheumatism. The chapel is really too cold for the older nuns to kneel in for long, but things like that we cannot heed. These are afflictions sent by God to help us cleanse our souls. After Sister Paul had shuffled out, we began to speak again. I was determined not to whisper because I didn't want Sister Agnes to get the idea that she had anything to hide from me.

" 'Why would she tell you to do this?' I asked.

" 'Because I'm getting fat,' Agnes replied.

"It was so preposterous an answer that I couldn't help getting annoyed, and I burst out at her.

" 'I am,' Agnes insisted. 'There's too much flesh on me. I'm a blimp,' she said, yet she couldn't have weighed more than a hundred pounds. If that.

"I was not only annoyed, but I was also puzzled. I asked her 'Why it would matter whether she was fat or not,' and she just said, 'Because.'

"Not for the first time, it struck me how much younger than her chronological age Agnes really was. I deliberately softened my voice, as you do when you're talking to a child.

" 'You needn't worry about being attractive here," I told her.

" 'I do,' she insisted, turning those huge eyes on me. 'I have to be attractive to God.'

" 'He loves you as you are.'

"But she shook her head from side to side, almost violently. 'No, He doesn't. He hates fat people.'

" 'Who told you this?' Now I was completely at sea, and further from understanding Agnes than I had ever been. Is she delusional? Is she hallucinating from near-starvation? Is this some religious form of anorexia?

" 'It's a sin to be fat,' she said.

" 'Why?'

" 'Look at all the statues. *They're* thin.' She smiled as she gazed at them, her face lit by more than candles.

"I looked at the statues as though seeing them for the first time. These are the saints we pray to, some of them martyrs. The statues are old, older than the convent, and were sent to us by the mother house in France. They stand to either side of the altar, and all are carved of wood and painted.

"There is a beautiful statue of the Blessed Virgin, to whom all of us pray daily. And, of course, Saint Marie Magdalen, whose name our order carries. She's kneeling at the feet of Christ crucified. And Saint Therese of Lisieux, our French saint. Saint Agnes the Martyr, who died under torture. Saint Sebastian, whom the Romans shot full of arrows. Saint Francis, who fed the animals, the gentle saint everyone loves. We put whatever flowers are in season on the base of the statues every second day. We also light candles when we say our prayers. There are tall candlesticks in front of the statues; they hold heavy beeswax candles that cast their light into the chapel. The chapel isn't as bright as it used to be, when there were so many more sisters to light candles with their prayers.

" 'Look at them, Reverend Mother. See how thin they are. That's because they're suffering. Suffering is beautiful. I want to be beautiful,' Agnes told me.

"For the first time, I was afraid for Agnes. Her mind seemed so simple, yet I couldn't recognize what was in it. 'Who tells you these things?' I asked her again.

"But Agnes was caught up in some private vision. She didn't even hear me. Finally she said, 'Christ said it in the Bible. He said, "Suffer the little children." I want to suffer like a little child.'

"I thought it strange that she would so mistake the definition of the word, confusing Jesus's meaning of *allow* with the pain of real suffering. It's the kind of mistake that children are always making. But a nun?

" 'That's not what He meant ...' I began, but Agnes was jumping to her feet, her eyes feverish, her hands still hidden in her habit. Her voice, usually pitched so low you can hardly hear it, grew louder.

" 'I *am* a little child, but my body keeps getting bigger and soon I won't be able to fit in. I won't be able to squeeze into heaven,' she told me with tears in her eyes; she really *was* suffering.

" 'Agnes, dear, heaven is not a place with bars you have to squeeze through, or doors or windows ...' I began, but Agnes wasn't listening to me at all. With her right hand, she grabbed at her two small breasts, her face twisted in a mask of disgust. The light of the candles burnished the gold of her nun's wedding band, symbol of her marriage with God.

" 'I mean, look at these! I've got to lose weight! I'm a blimp!' Her hand tore angrily at her breasts.

"I was so stunned that I had to force myself to stand up and move toward her, trying to comfort her, but she backed away from me as though she didn't recognize me, and I could take my oath that at that moment she didn't. Her face was distorted by a nameless fear. This was an Agnes I had never seen before, although perhaps I had seen a hint of her, a hint I'd never wanted to acknowledge. She backed down the aisle, and she was close to hysteria. She actually babbled.

" 'God blew up the Hindenburg, He'll blow up me!' That's what she said!

" 'Who!' I yelled.

" 'Mummy!' she yelled back. 'I'll get bigger and bigger every day and then I'll pop. But if I stay little it won't happen!'

"I couldn't believe my ears. 'Your mother tells you this?' I asked her, but at the mention of her mother, Agnes froze as though she'd said too much, given away her most carefully guarded secret. Her mouth dropped open as if she was in shock. I took a step toward her; she took a step back. I took another step, and so did she. She stared at me, but she didn't see me; she seemed to be seeing through me as through a pane of glass. I didn't take another step. I wanted her out of this hysteria, out of this nightmare of hers. You know how they say it's dangerous to wake a sleepwalker? At that moment it seemed to me that Agnes was very like a sleepwalker, and I was afraid to wake her.

"I spoke to her gently, but firmly. 'Agnes dear, your mother is dead.'

"She nodded knowingly. 'But she watches. She listens.' Could she really believe that? I wondered.

"I tried another tack. 'Nonsense. I'm your mother now, and I want you to eat.'

" 'I'm not hungry.'

" 'You have to eat something, Agnes.'

"She shook her head. 'No, I don't. The Host is enough.'

"I don't know why, but this struck me as ludicrous. 'My dear,' I told her, 'I don't think a communion wafer has the Recommended Daily Allowance of *anything.'*

" 'Of God,' Agnes said, and she was quite serious.

"I stood corrected. No argument there. 'Oh, yes, of God.'

"I noticed for the first time that Agnes was staring, terrified, down at her feet. I followed her gaze and saw a puddle of blood on the floor at her feet, not large, but still forming.

"I didn't know where it came from and there was also a large red stain forming on Agnes's white scapular, just under the dangling crucifix, where her left hand was still hidden.

" 'Agnes, what is it?'

"Now she saw the stain on her scapular, the red leaking through the white linen, growing, spreading. Her face was a mask of terror, and she took a large step back, nearly knocking down the candlestick in front of Saint Sebastian.

" 'I'm being punished,' she told me; she was close to tears.

" 'For what?'

" 'I don't know!' she wailed, like a stricken infant.

"I rushed at her and ripped the scapular to one side, grabbing at her hidden hand, which she held palm upward, the blood seeping steadily through the fingers.

" 'Oh, dear Jesus,' I whispered hoarsely. There was a hole in the palm of Agnes's hand, a hole that was bleeding heavily.

" 'It started this morning, and I can't get it to stop,' she sobbed. 'Why me, Mother? Why me?'

"And I had no answer to give her." The nun stopped speaking, utterly drained, her shoulders drooping in weariness, her hands slack at her sides.

"Why didn't you send her to a doctor?" demanded Dr. Livingston.

Mother Miriam Ruth turned from the cross-shaped shadow on the wall. "It was healed by the following morning. She began eating again, and that seemed the most important thing at the time . . . besides, the wound never came back."

"She had a hole in the palm of her hand! She could have bled to death!" shouted Martha, exploding.

"But she didn't, did she?" The mother superior's fury matched the doctor's. "If anyone else had seen what I had seen, she'd be public property. Newspapers, psychiatrists, ridicule. She doesn't deserve that!"

Martha drew a deep breath. "Well, she has it now," she said quietly. Inside her head, the voice that clamored "Marie! Marie!" was making itself heard again.

"I know what you're thinking," said Mother Miriam Ruth. "She's an hysteric, pure and simple."

"Not simple, no."

"I saw it! Clean through the palm of her hand! Do you think hysteria did that?"

"It's been doing it for centuries, hasn't it? Saint

Francis of Assisi and Saint Catherine of Siena, to
name only two. And what about the thousands
who *weren't* saints, whose wounds had nothing to
do with sanctity, just religious obsession! She's
not unique, she's just another victim!"

"Yes, God's victim!" retorted the mother superior hotly. "*That's* her innocence. She belongs
to God!"

"And I mean to take her away from Him?
That's what you fear, isn't it?" demanded the
psychiatrist.

"You bet I do!"

They glared at each other, their anger out in
the open, the battle lines between them drawn
clear. To Dr. Livingston, religion was the drug to
which this adolescent girl was addicted and upon
which her morbid Freudian fantasies fed. A
wretched childhood at the hands of an obviously
psychotic mother combined with the mysticism
of the Church, its rituals, and the unnatural qual-
ities of the celibate life all contributed to a sexual hysteria that barred the way to Agnes's
acceptance of reality.

To Mother Miriam Ruth, Sister Agnes was
cast in the mold of the saints and martyrs who
had received the stigmata, the wounds of Christ.
She was something to cherish and to protect from
the outside world. The mother superior's belief
in the innocence of Agnes was blinding. It had
been she who had found the baby's body, she
who had given its bloody little head the sacra-
ment of baptism, yet somehow she had eradi-

cated the killing from her consciousness almost as effectively as Agnes had.

Agnes dei, thought Martha bitterly. *Lamb of God. Yet who had led this lamb to the slaughter?*

Six

"Would you tell me why the hell this is taking so long?" Eugene Lyon chewed savagely at his cigar and scowled, oblivious to the view of downtown Montreal that was visible through the tall window of the judge's courthouse chambers. As defense attorney for the accused, he was impatient; secure in his opinion that a nun who gives birth in secret to a baby and then strangles it must be insane. He was convinced that any psychiatrist must agree with his opinion almost sight unseen, and he was eager to present the insanity findings and move for dismissal. Besides, his fee was being paid by the Church, and the Church wanted its money's worth.

"Look, there are a lot of unanswered questions here. . . ." Dr. Livingston began defensively.

"Your job is to diagnose, not to heal and not to play detective," snarled Lyon.

Stung, Martha responded in anger. "I know my job. Don't tell me my job. My duty as a doctor—"

"Martha," said the Crown attorney, Eve LeClaire LeClaire, wearily, "you're to make a decision on her sanity as quickly as possible and not interfere with due process of law."

"As quickly as I see fit," corrected the psychiatrist. Why am I always put on the defensive by these men, she asked herself. My professional qualifications are as good as theirs. My experience is as valid. Why then do I always seem to be standing here in the center of the room like a deer facing the hounds, while they sit on their asses in those damn leather chairs in a circle around me, like barking dogs? Or am I getting paranoid? They want this case to come to a rapid conclusion. What do they think I want? I never wanted to take this case in the first place, but I'm sure as hell not going to let them give me the royal rush just to wind it up.

"The longer you take to make a decision, the more difficult it will be for me," continued LeClaire.

"Why?"

"The bishop is breathing down our goddamned necks!"

"So the sooner she's in prison, the better off she'll be?" demanded Martha sarcastically.

Justice Leveau put up one soothing hand. "Mar-

tha, whatever your decision, I'm going to allow
her to return to the convent and serve her time
there."

This was morally and legally incredible! Eyes
flashing, she wheeled on the judge. "I don't believe this!" she gasped. "I don't bloody believe
this!"

"You wouldn't recommend that she be returned
to the convent?" asked the judge, without rais-
ing his voice.

"I wouldn't send her back to the source of her
problem, no," retorted Martha.

"The bishop will be very upset about this,"
warned Lyon.

Now it was Lyon upon whom the psychiatrist
turned her angry face. "I'm fighting for this woman's life, not for any bloody bishop!" she cried. It
was science against religion, that age-old conflict, and science would always be losing its al-
lies when religion had so much political power.
Unfortunately, Martha couldn't bring that out
into the open as the real issue here. There were
some things you didn't dare say if you wanted to
remain effective. Besides, these men would deny
it, and it was quite possible that they didn't
perceive it as an issue after all.

If you look at it in a certain way, there's not so
much difference between a convent and a nursing home, thought Martha as she parked the car
in the concrete parking lot and made her way up
the front steps. They are both shut away from

the world; both create an artificial society into which nothing from the outside, real world is allowed to penetrate; nothing changes from day to day because nothing is allowed to change; and the customary release is death. She shivered. She hated coming here, telling herself every time she visited that this was the best place for her mother to be, the only way she could be looked after on a round-the-clock basis. Nevertheless, she hated it.

The smell always got her first. Compounded of antiseptics, urine, feces, and industrial-strength cleaners, it hit her in the face as soon as she walked into the reception area and signed the visitors' book. It was a smell she had come naturally to associate with her mother, and just as naturally she felt guilty for doing so.

Carrying the little white paper bag in her hand, Martha headed for the day room, where the television set was always on. Her mother was usually sitting there, watching TV, and she was there now. Gratefully, Martha took out a cigarette and lit it. The day room was the only place in the nursing home where you were allowed to smoke.

About half a dozen patients, most of them in wheelchairs, sat around the room, facing the set, but only one or two were actually watching. A couple were asleep, one was crying desolately, and another was moaning as though her heart would break, while long strings of spittle crept down her chin. Having learned from experience

that nothing she could say or do would help the
moaner or the crier, who were shut tightly away
inside their own heads, the psychiatrist went
directly to her mother, who sat nearest the set,
wrapped in a stained robe, her hair uncombed,
her face unwashed. Martha leaned over the chair
and kissed her with great tenderness.

"Hi, Mama."

The old woman turned to look up at her, then
turned back at once to the TV. A brightly colored animated cartoon, filled with violence, was
"zapping" and "powing" on the box. Martha knelt
beside her mother's chair.

"I brought you something." Martha held out
the paper bag.

"Shut up," the old woman said crossly. "I'm
trying to watch this." She grinned emptily at the
screen, where a superhero in a spider costume
had just whammed a yellow-faced enemy.

Taking the container out of the bag, Martha
pried off the lid and fished for the plastic spoon.
Her mother threw a sidelong glance at the ice
cream, then grabbed it out of Martha's hand without a word. She dug in and began to eat greedily.

"It's your favorite," Martha said.

"Who are you?" asked the old woman.

"It's Martha, Mama."

"Marie brings me ice cream, too, you know.
Chocolate. My favorite." Her eyes narrowed in
fuzzy recollection.

Marie is dead, Mama. That was me who brought
you the chocolate ice cream. Me, Mama, Martha

wanted to say. "I thought cherry vanilla was your favorite."

The old woman took another bite. "Not anymore. Now I like chocolate."

"Have you had a nice week?" the psychiatrist asked. "Are they taking good care of you?"

But her mother wasn't listening. "You know," she confided, her mouth sticky with the ice cream, "Martha never comes to see me. You watch it, she's going straight to hell. After all the things she said to me. And then she marries that son-of-a-bitch of a Frenchman. I knew that wasn't gonna work out. Not like you, Marie. You got married to God."

"Marie's dead, Mama," said Martha softly.

The old woman laughed. "I remember when you were a little girl, Marie, you'd come back from the movies and you'd say, 'Mama, that ending was so sad,' and I'd tell you they had all the happy endings locked away in a vault in Hollywood. And you believed me." Chuckling, she paid no attention to the ice cream dribbling out of her mouth and down her chin.

That wasn't Marie, Mama. That was me. When did this happen to you, Mama? You were always so strong, so tough, so smart. Why does this happen to us? She knew how and why, of course. She was a doctor, wasn't she? She could deliver a lecture on the hardening of the arteries, the diminishing blood supply to the brain, the increasing disorientation, loss of memory, the confusion of identities, the retreat from reality. Facts.

Dr. Martha Livingston's beloved scientific facts.
But what good were facts in the face of suffer-
ing? Where was reason when reason had fled?
"That wasn't Marie, Mama. That was me."
"Who are you?"

Part of her wanted to go back to the convent at
once, day after day until the mystery was solved,
until Agnes the lamb of God yielded up her secrets. Part of her never wanted to go back again.
The convent made her acutely uncomfortable; it
was a world she despised, inhabited by a race of
women she couldn't understand. The life of a
cloistered religious woman seemed to her to be
the ultimate denial of life, and a festering breed-
ing ground for the exact type of hysteria of which
Sister Agnes was the victim.

In the seventeenth century an entire convent
of French nuns, recalled Martha, had been gripped
by a sexual frenzy, obsessed with the idea that
they were copulating with devils, and a priest
had paid for that obsession with his life. Aldous
Huxley had put the grim episode into a book,
The Devils of Loudon. And in the same century,
in Salem, Massachusetts, a group of adolescent
girls, apparently unable to deal with their newly
emerging sexuality, had fantasized about witches,
and a group of harmless old women had gone to
the gallows. Agnes appeared to be the perfect
candidate for that kind of classic obsession. All
the elements were already present in her, a de-
layed adolescence, a loathing for and fear of the

physical functions, and a piety and mysticism
that amounted almost to religious mania.

But had she already been pushed over the edge
into madness? *That* Dr. Livingston had not yet
decided. And it was odd. Away from the convent, Martha could bring all her vaunted intelligence and rationality, all her Freudian theories,
to bear on the case. But once inside those stone
walls, once she was talking to Agnes, listening to
Agnes, those theories seemed to fly out of the
Gothic window and all that remained was the
purity of Agnes's presence, the innocence in her
eyes. Martha was beginning to understand why
Mother Miriam Ruth was so protective of the
young nun.

It seemed to Martha that she, too, was beginning to lose sight of the dead baby, of the terrible
act that had brought her to this convent time
after time. At Martha's request, Richard Langevin
had requisitioned a set of police photographs
of the crime scene. She forced herself to examine
the horrific pictures of the slain infant in detail,
impressing upon her memory the atrocity in the
pictures.

She was back at the convent today, yet another
visit to probe into the girl's psyche and dredge
up . . . what?

The month was drawing to a close, the weather
turning colder. But in the late afternoon, the
wind was stilled, and the sun still held the power
of warmth. Stifled by the convent walls, Martha
had suggested that they walk out of doores, and

Agnes had agreed joyfully. She wanted to visit the convent cemetery, to pay her respects to the grave of the late Sister Paul.

The graveyard was close by the chapel, a simple, pastoral burying ground. No marble mausoleums with seraphs weeping at the corners, no gilded statues of the Angel Gabriel sounding the trumpet of the Day of Judgment. The graves were marked by plain headstones, just the name and the dates—such pitiful facts—and a little cross marked INRI, Jesus, born the King of the Jews, that mocking phrase of His Roman executioners. The only statue in the graveyard was of Mother Mary, and the graves were grouped around her as though seeking her wisdom and her comfort even in death.

Sister Agnes knelt down by one of these graves, crossed herself and whispered a short prayer. The headstone was a recent one, inscribed *"Soeur Marie Paul, Born July 21, 1898, Died January 23, 1984."*

"You liked Sister Paul," said Dr. Livingston gently.

"She was kind to me. She told me I was beautiful," answered Agnes.

"What else did she tell you?" Martha had positioned herself behind Agnes, so that she could observe the girl without confronting her; also, she felt as always the need to smoke.

"She said all of God's angels would want to sleep beside me if they could." Agnes leaned over and scraped the dead leaves away from the

tombstone and laid on the grave the little bunch
of autumn flowers she'd been carrying, a few
asters and mums, and one or two late-blooming
zinnias that hadn't been killed by the night frost.

"I liked that," she continued. "She lived here
for over seventy years, and every day she rang
the bell, to wake us up, to call us to God . . . She
took me to my secret place," she added shyly.

All of Martha's senses wakened to the alert.
"Where's that?" she asked as casually as she
could. But Agnes averted her face, her eyes cast
down. Yet she smiled, as though she wanted to
share her secret with the doctor.

"Take me there," urged Martha softly. "I promise I won't tell." And was rewarded with the
smallest nod.

It was a long climb upward. The steps were
narrow and steep, and Martha felt herself becoming out of breath as she followed Agnes up
and up to the bell tower.

"Sister Paul was in her eighties, wasn't she?
Did she climb up here often?" she panted.

"No, only when she felt like it. She brought
me here last winter, and the next day she died."

"No wonder," murmured Martha to herself.
She tried to catch her breath. Above her on the
stairs, Sister Agnes climbed like a young mountain goat, skipping lightly from step to step. I
must be getting old, she thought. "Agnes, how do
you feel about babies?"

"Oh, they frighten me. I'm afraid I'll drop
them. They have a soft spot on their heads, and

if you drop them so they land on their heads, they become stupid. That's where I was dropped. I don't understand things," she confided.

"Like what?" Had Agnes really been dropped on her head, or was this one more cruel joke played on a defenseless child?

Agnes shrugged a little. "Numbers. You could spend your whole life counting and never reach the end."

"I don't understand them either," confessed the doctor, smiling. "Do you think I was dropped on my head?" she joked.

But Agnes took her literally, as she took everything literally. "I hope not," she said solemnly, with an anxious look at Martha. "It's a terrible thing to be dropped on your head."

They had reached the bell tower, an old, square structure with open archways on all four sides— unglassed windows open to the elements. Hanging by ropes from the tower's lofty ceiling was the bell, and beneath the bell a sturdy platform on which the bell could rest. Birds—mourning doves—had nested in the tower, and their droppings were congealed on the walls, but their nests had been long abandoned as the birds had migrated to warmer climates.

The bell itself was very beautiful. Cast of bronze a century before, it was engraved with angels, on its outside and inside, and around the rim was carved a sentence in Latin: *Sum Vox Angelorum*—I am the Voice of Angels.

The sun had traveled the sky to the west and

was hanging low over the far horizon. The western sky was colored brightly by long streaks of pink, purple, and gold, and the cloud formations were a brilliant orange, dyed by the sun's last rays. From the bell tower, one could see for miles, over the countryside dotted with farms and villages, over the treetops and the steeples of the churches. It was breathtaking, a landscape of dreams lit by a dying sun.

"Sister Paul said I could see the whole world from up here," said Agnes softly. "That it looks much better from far away than it does up close."

"It's beautiful," agreed Martha, awed by the view.

Making her way onto the bell platform, Sister Agnes lay on her back directly under the bell so that she could peer up into its brazen depths. "And sometimes I'll crawl under here and sing. It makes a wonderful sound!" Taking a deep breath, she sang a long note. The sound echoed back, filling the tower with its music and drifting through the window openings. Agnes laughed like a child.

"What happens if the bell rings and you're under there?" Martha wanted to know.

"It's even more wonderful then." Agnes smiled

The psychiatrist stepped gingerly onto the platform and squeezed under the bell, sitting next to Agnes. Both of them laughed, rather like conspirators sharing a powerful secret.

"It's like hiding from my mother when I was a little girl," said the doctor.

"Where did *you* go?" Agnes asked.

"No place as wonderful as this." For a minute, they sat in silence, side by side. Their companionship was total, as though they were bound together by ties of kinship. Sisters? No, the age difference between them would make them mother and daughter. Is this what it's like to have a child? wondered Martha. This sense of silent communication? How rare it must be, but how utterly fulfilling. And she felt a pang of loss.

Above them, the interior of the bell cupped them as though they were together in a little house, or perhaps even a womb. A single ray of light came from inside the top of the bell, from the stem of the clapper, lighting up the carvings of the angels.

"Agnes, have you ever thought of leaving the convent? For something else?"

The girl shook her head decisively. "Oh, no, there's nothing else. Just being here helps me sleep at night."

"You have trouble sleeping?" Martha asked carefully.

"I get headaches. Mummy did, too. Oh, but she wasn't stupid. She knew things nobody else knows."

"What things?"

"She knew what was going to happen to me, and that's why she hid me away."

Martha felt her pulses beating. This was the closest she had come so far. Was it possible that Agnes could be on the verge of some revelation, of telling her something significant, something that might make all the puzzle pieces fit together? Carefully, not too fast, Martha knew she had to go softly and not frighten her. Agnes finally seemed to be accepting her as a friend.

"How did she know?"

"Somebody told her," said Agnes ingenuously.

"Who?"

"I don't know."

But it was evident that she *did* know. And that she wanted to tell. "Agnes," prompted the doctor.

The girl shook her head. "You'll laugh."

"I promise I won't laugh. Who told her?"

Agnes turned her face to Martha. "An angel," she said. "When she was having one of her headaches."

"Did your mother see angels often?"

"No."

"Do you?"

"No," Agnes answered, but too quickly. The psychiatrist decided to retreat from that for a minute. "Do you believe your mother really saw them?"

"No," Sister Agnes said slowly, "but I could never tell her that."

"Why not?"

The nun's face darkened. "She'd get angry," she said in a tight voice. "She'd punish me."

"How would she punish you?" Dr. Livingston sought the girl's eyes with her own, and her words were so quietly spoken that only the fact that the two of them were cupped inside the resonant bell allowed them to be heard.

But Agnes avoided her eyes. Whatever it was that she was remembering, it was too bitter a thought to dwell on or share with Martha. "She'd . . . punish me," she muttered, and crawled out from under the bell, moving away from the doctor to one of the open arches.

Dr. Livingston, too, left the shelter of the bell but made no move to follow the young nun. Instead, she remained on the platform and lit up a cigarette. Her heart was pounding hard in excitement, but she had to appear calm and natural. If she betrayed her eagerness, Agnes might be scared off, destroying the first real bond of communication between them.

"Did you love your mother?" She changed tack, steering a perilous course without a chart.

"Oh, yes! Yes!" Agnes smiled.

"Did you ever want to become a mother yourself?" We must get back to the baby. Somehow I must get her to talk about the baby.

"I could never be a mother." The girl frowned, and her grayish eyes darkened to a navy blue.

"Why not?"

"I don't think I'm old enough. Besides, I don't want a baby."

"Why not?" Martha asked again.

"Because I don't want one." The girl's face set stubbornly, in an expression Dr. Livingston had not seen before.

Softly. Be casual. "But if you did want one, how would you go about getting one?"

"From someone who didn't want a baby," answered Sister Agnes promptly.

"Like you?"

"No! Not like me!" The shake of the cowled head was vehement.

"But how would that person get the baby if they didn't want it?"

"A mistake." The girl's nose wrinkled in distaste.

Martha held her breath. "How did your mother get you?"

"A mistake! It was a mistake!" cried Agnes, and her mouth trembled like a child's on the verge of tears.

"Is that what she said?"

The girl's hands clenched and unclenched nervously. She was shouting now, her face dark with anger. "You're trying to get me to say that she was a bad woman," she flung at the psychiatrist, "and that she hated me and didn't want me, but that is not true! She was a good woman, a saint! You don't want to hear the nice parts about her!"

This display of wrath the doctor saw as a positive thing, a release of genuine emotion and a breach in the girl's careful defenses. This was the moment she had been waiting for. Now perhaps Martha could get her to open up further, to lay bare the facts surrounding the mystery. Perhaps the force of Agnes's anger would unlock the truth. Martha began moving slowly toward the young nun, who kept backing away.

"Agnes, I cannot imagine that you know nothing about sex . . ."

"I can't help it if I'm stupid!" the girl shouted.

"Or that you have no remembrance of your impregnation . . ."

"It's not my fault!" Agnes cried.

"And that you don't believe you carried a child!"

"It was a mistake!" The girl's voice rose to a shriek, ending in a wail.

"What, the child?" Martha pressed her, unrelenting.

"Everything! Nuns don't have children!" she sobbed brokenly.

Dr. Livingston reached out to her with her right hand, the hand that held the cigarette. The sight of the burning cigarette made Agnes recoil in terror, and she lashed out at Martha's outstretched hand.

"Don't touch me like that! Don't touch me like that!" Her screams held genuine fear.

The recoil set the girl off balance, and she swayed for a moment, perilously near the open arch of the tower wall. Instantly, Martha grabbed for her, pulling her back to safety.

But Agnes tore herself from Martha's protective grip as though the doctor was contaminated by Satan. Instinctively, her hand reached up to grasp the crucifix that hung around her neck, and rested on the white scapular of her habit.

"I know what you want from me!" she cried, close to hysterical. "I know what you want from me!" she cried, close to hysterical. "You want to take God away! You should be ashamed! They should lock *you* up, people like you!" She whirled and ran down the stairs.

The psychiatrist could only stare after her, confused and more than a little hurt. Was the girl right? *Was* she trying to take God from Agnes? In her own passion for the rational, for the scientifically explicable, was she trying to rob this girl of something just as precious to *her*—her emotional home in the breast of Christ? All she wanted was for Agnes to come out from behind the barrier of mysticism she had erected against the truth so painstakingly, to face reality. And if she succeeded in bringing Agnes into the real world, might there not be a terrible price they both would have to pay?

Seven

The mother superior was cold with anger. Seeing Agnes in tears had awakened in her all her protective instincts. When Dr. Livingston came into her office, Mother Miriam Ruth was ready for her. With the gloves off.

"What did you say to Sister Agnes?" she demanded.

"I asked her some questions. That's what I'm here for, isn't it?" countered the psychiatrist defensively. "To get at the truth?"

The two women confronted each other in the near-darkness of the room. The convent relied as little as possible on the outside world, and that included the power company. If they could have dispensed with electricity entirely, they would have done so gladly. But it was too late for that, in the last two decades of the twentieth century. So they used electric light sparingly, and the mother superior's office was lit only by a single desk lamp, which threw grotesque shadows on the walls of the room and illuminated the women's faces from below.

"You hate us, don't you?" asked Mother Miriam Ruth suddenly.

Martha was caught entirely off her guard, as the nun had intended. "What!" she cried.

"Nuns. You hate nuns."

"I hate ignorance and stupidity," the psychiatrist replied uncomfortably.

"And the Catholic Church," accused the mother superior.

Martha was on shaky ground here, and she knew it. Nevertheless, she attempted a denial. "I haven't said a word against the—"

But Mother Miriam Ruth cut her off decisively. "This is a human being you're dealing with, not an institution."

Martha put her back up. "But the institution has a hell of a lot to do with—"

It was obvious that the mother superior was not about to let her finish. "Catholicism is not on trial here," she said sternly. "I want you to deal with Agnes without any religious prejudices or turn this case over to another psychiatrist."

"How dare you tell me how to run my affairs!" shouted Martha, furious.

"It's my affair, too!" the nun shouted back, equally furious.

The two women exploded at each other, shouting at the tops of their voices, interrupting each other, each of them determined to get her point across without hearing the other's arguments. It seemed to both of them that the fate of Sister Agnes hung in the balance here, awaiting the outcome of this argument, and nothing else.

"How *dare* you think that I'm in a position to be pressured . . ." raged Martha.

"I'm only requesting that you be fair," countered the mother superior.

"Or bullied or whatever you're trying to do. Who the hell do you think you are? You walk around here high and mighty, expecting applause for the way you've treated this child?"

"She's not a child," stated Mother Miriam Ruth flatly.

"And she has a right to know!" continued Martha, unheeding. "That there is a world out there filled with people who don't believe in God and who are not any worse off than you! People who go through their entire lives without bending their knees once to anybody! And people who still fall in love, and make babies, and occasionally are very happy. She has a right to know that. But you and your order and your church have kept her ignorant . . ."

"We could hardly do that, even if we wanted—"

"Because ignorance is next to virginity, right? "Poverty, chastity, and ignorance! That's what you live by!"

"I am not a virgin, Doctor," said the mother superior quietly.

Martha's eyes snapped open in surprise, and the flow of her words was suddenly checked. Mother Miriam Ruth gave her little half smile at the amazed expression on Dr. Livingston's usually self-contained face.

Opening the top drawer of her desk, the mother superior pulled out a small double picture frame. "I was married for twenty-three years. Two daughters." She tossed the frame on the desk as evidence. The faces of two young women smiled up at the speechless psychiatrist. "I even have grandchildren. Surprised?"

One look at Dr. Livingston told her how effective her sudden announcement had been. Satisfied, Mother Miriam Ruth placed the frame gently back and shut the drawer.

"It might please you to know," she continued, "that I was a failure as a wife and mother. Possibly because I protected my children from nothing. They won't see me anymore. That's their revenge. I think they tell their friends I've passed on. Oh, don't tell me, Dr. Freud, that I'm making up for past mistakes."

But Martha was shaking her head; that was not what she intended to say, not even what she was thinking. She was thinking that Mother Miriam Ruth, having been a wife and mother, should have an even greater depth of understanding than a woman who had been celibate her entire life.

"You can help her," she began earnestly, her blue eyes probing the nun's brown ones.

"I am helping her. With everything within my power."

"No," she said urgently, "you're shielding her. Let her face the big bad world."

"Meaning you?" Mother Miriam Ruth cocked an eyebrow tinged with faint sarcasm.

"If that's what you think, yes," answered Martha simply.

"What good would it do?" the nun cried out. "No matter what you decide, it's either the prison or the nut house, and the differences between them are pretty thin." Her lips twisted bitterly, and she suddenly looked much older, older even than her years.

"There's another choice," said Martha slowly.

"What's that?"

"Acquittal." The word surprised her as it came out of her mouth.

Hope flared up in the nun's dark eyes, then turned to suspicion. "How?" she demanded.

"Innocence. Legal innocence. I know the judge would be happy for *any* reason to throw this case out of court."

There was a silence as the mother superior thought over the psychiatrist's words, a silence in which hope was reborn.

"What do you need?" said Mother Miriam Ruth.

"Answers."

"Ask." An unspoken, uneasy truce was formed between them.

Martha pulled her cigarettes and her notebook out of her big leather purse. She lit up and riffled through the pages of her notes. "When would Agnes have conceived the child?"

"Sometime in January."

"You don't remember anything unusual happening at that time?"

The eyebrow rose again. "Earthquakes?" asked Mother Miriam Ruth dryly.

"Visitors at the convent."

The nun shook her head. "Nothing."

"Do you keep a diary? A daybook?"

"Yes."

"Look at it."

"I have."

"Look again."

Mother Miriam Ruth opened the side drawer of her desk and rummaged around in it. A small cluster of ledgers was kept there for quick reference, account books, lists of supplies, and, at last, the correct one, the daybook, not unlike a ship captain's log. Setting it on the desk before her, she sat down and began to flip through the pages until she came to the approximate dates that might be of concern. Then she began to pay closer attention. Even so, she was shaking her head.

"There's nothing here."

"Was the child full-term?" asked Dr. Livingston.

Suddenly, the mother superior's eyes widened as she noticed something that had not registered before. "Oh, dear God," she breathed as she began to flip back the pages.

Martha sat up straight. "What is it?"

Mother Miriam Ruth didn't look up or respond. Instead, she was going through the book a page at a time, her fingers trembling. "The sheets," she muttered.

"What sheets?"

"Dear God, I should have known. I should have suspected something. . . ."

"Tell me!" cried Martha. "It's imperative that I know!"

"Yes," replied Mother Miriam Ruth slowly, "I suppose it is. I suppose you have the right to know." She pushed the daybook aside as though it were contaminated and bit at her lower lip thoughtfully, trying to bring the entire story up out of the recesses of her memory.

The doctor leaned forward in her chair, her eyes intent on the older woman's face.

"We'd received communion from Father Martineau at vespers. I had intended to speak to Sister Agnes early in the day, but I changed my mind. For purely selfish reasons, I suspect. I think that, whatever reason I gave myself for my delay, it was simply because I didn't want to upset her before the evening service. She sings magnificently, you know. A voice from heaven. I think I wanted to hear her singing the Gloria and the Credo and the responses. Besides, she always looks forward to Father Martineau's weekly visits and the Mass. She loves going to confession with him; did she tell you that?"

"Yes, she did," said Martha very softly.

"Now it all comes back to me, so very clearly," Mother Miriam Ruth continued. "We had eaten the evening meal; the priest had gone back to the village. The nuns were cleaning up the dishes and folding the white cloth, but I nodded my head for Agnes to remain seated. I meant to talk to her, to question her, and bring this thing she was hiding out into the open. She was still a novice then; she had not yet taken her final vows.

"An important part of convent life is the fact that we are a community, with no secrets from one another. A nun's life is an open book. We all live by the same rules, following the same prescribed daily routine; what can any one of us have to hide from her sisters in Christ? Therefore, when a nun—any nun—is seen by another to deviate in any way from our routine, it is the other nun's duty to bring the aberration to the attention of the mother superior. And it is the duty of the mother superior to question the sister in the presence of the other sisters, so that all may share and benefit in the mother superior's instruction.

"I spoke to her with some severity, since this was to be a public chastisement. 'Sister Marguerite tells me you've been sleeping on a bare mattress, Sister. Is this true?'

"Aware that everybody was looking at her, Agnes bowed her head and her pale face turned red with embarrassment.

"She said, 'Yes, Mother,' in a voice so low I could barely hear her.

" 'Why?'

" 'In medieval days nuns and monks would sleep in their coffins,' whispered Agnes."

"For God's sake!" Martha couldn't help her exclamation, and the mother superior threw her a wry look.

"That's just about what Sister Marguerite said, along with a snort of derision, but I threw her a look that shut her up. 'We're not in the Middle Ages, Sister,' I told Agnes.

" 'It made them holy,' Agnes replied. She can be damn stubborn.

" 'It made them uncomfortable. If they didn't sleep well, I'm certain that the next day they were cranky as mules,' I told her. Out of the corner of my eye I looked at Sister Marguerite, who, I think, got the message. Then I turned my full attention back to Sister Agnes.

" 'Sister, where are your sheets?'

"She evaded my eyes and said nothing. Something was very definitely wrong, but I didn't know what.

" 'Do you really believe that sleeping on a bare mattress is the equivalent of sleeping in a coffin?'

" 'No,' she admitted, but very faintly. I knew she really hated this cross-examination, especially in public. However, I couldn't do otherwise, and

Sister Agnes (Meg Tilly) is a young nun accused of bearing and then murdering her newborn child in a convent.

Dr. Martha Livingston (Jane Fonda) and Richard Langevin (Winston Reckart) discuss the case in which Livingston has become as much of a detective as a court psychiatrist.

Sister Agnes sings with a pure, angelic voice that transports her listeners as well as herself.

Mother Miriam Ruth (Anne Bancroft), who believes
Sister Agnes is touched by God, confronts Dr.
Livingston, who believes Agnes is a patient in need of
healing.

When Agnes and Martha build a friendship, Agnes takes
the doctor to the grave of her dearest friend, Sister Paul.

After visiting Sister Paul's grave, Agnes feels even closer to Martha Livingtson.

Mother Miriam Ruth witnesses Agnes's stigmata.

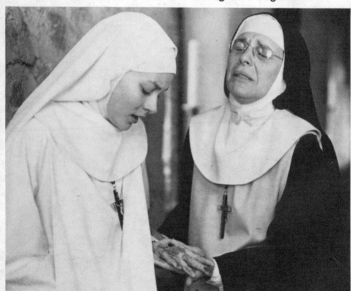

Having learned of an underground passage leading from the convent to the barn, Dr. Livingston retraces what she believes were Agnes's steps the night she conceived her child.

Dr. Livingtson hypnotizes Sister Agnes in the hope of learning more about the events leading up to the nun's child's birth.

Under hypnosis, Agnes tells of the night Sister Paul, on her deathbed, revealed to Agnes where she could meet with God.

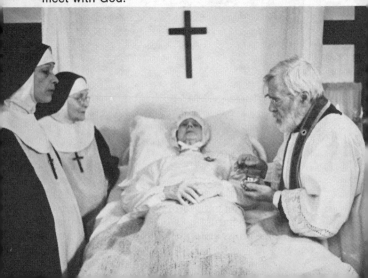

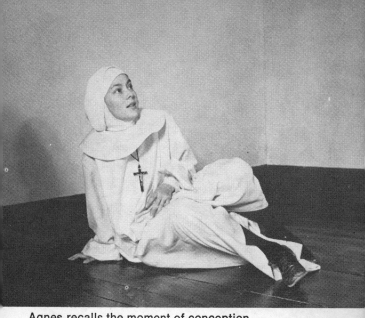

Agnes recalls the moment of conception . . .

Standing in the sun-bathed barn, Agnes recalls seeing a marvelous light shine upon her and feels she has meet God, as Sister Paul said she would.

Until the very last moment, Mother Miriam Ruth
continues to believe in Agnes's innocence.

Sister Agnes addresses the court at her hearing,
recalling her visitation from God.

I was determined to get to the bottom of the matter.

" 'Then tell me, where are your sheets?' I forced her to meet my eyes by the sheer strength of my will.

"Her cheeks red with shame, Agnes whispered, 'I burned them.'

" 'Why?'

" 'They were stained.'

"Everything became clear to me, and I was really irritated. There was nothing out of the ordinary here, in fact it was all too common, even in the world outside the convent. I stood up and raised my voice, so that everybody in the room heard me loud and clear.

" 'Sister, how many times have I burned into your thick skull and the thick skull of your fellow novice . . .' I looked hard at Sister Genevieve then, and the poor girl began to shake. 'That menstruation is a perfectly natural process and nothing to be ashamed of.'

" 'Yes, Mother,' whispered Agnes. She was mortified.

" 'Say it.' And I glared at both my little novices. Girls of that age tend to be self-conscious about their bodies and their natural functions. When you add to that a religious fervor and a call to God, you often get a girl who cannot deal with anything that smacks of the physical. It takes time and patience, but you can get them over it.

" 'It is a perfectly natural process,' Sister Agnes and Sister Genevieve chorused dutifully—they knew this by rote now—'and nothing to be ashamed of.' But I saw that their hearts weren't in it.

" 'Mean it!' I roared. A good mother superior has a lot of drill sergeant in her.''

"So I remember," murmured Martha, but the nun was caught up entirely in her recollections.

"They started again. 'It is a perfectly natural process . . .' At which point, Agnes broke down and started to cry.

"We aren't given to touching one another in the convent; at least, not very often, and not at all if we can help it. But Agnes was so ashamed and so confused, and I sensed something more. Could it have been fear? Why fear? And I have had children of my own, whom I held in my arms. So, unnatural as it is in convent life, I found it natural to go to Agnes and put one arm around her to give her a little temporal as well as spiritual reassurance.

" 'A few years ago one of our sisters came to me in tears, asking for comfort. Comfort because she was too old to have any children. Not that she intended to,' I told Agnes and smiled, 'but once a month she had been reminded of the possibility of motherhood. So dry your eyes, Sister, and thank God that he has filled you with this possibility.' "

A pang of something like shame mingled with bitterness suddenly attacked Martha. For her, the possibility was no longer there.

"But Agnes wouldn't look at me. She kept her eyes glued to the table, as though wishing she could hide inside the dark polished wood. Her fact started to twist, as though she was about to cry. 'It's not that. It's not that.' And she rocked her body back and forth.

" 'What do you mean?' I asked her.

" 'It's not my time of month.' I realized that she was dangerously close to tears.

"That began to worry me. Anorexia is bad enough, but midmonth bleeding can be an early warning of something far more dangerous.

" 'Should you see a doctor?' I asked her, swinging her around so that she had to look at me.

"Once she saw the worried look on my face, her fear poured out of her. 'I don't know,' she said, almost moaning. 'I don't know what happened, Mother. I woke up and there was blood on the sheets, but I don't understand what happened! I don't know what I did wrong! I don't know why I should be punished!' Tears spilled out of her eyes and down her cheeks; I had never seen her so miserably unhappy and afraid.

" 'Punished? For what?' I demanded.

" 'I don't know!' she sobbed, and the other nuns were frozen as if in a painted tableau, staring at the two of us. Agnes clung to me, weeping loudly.

" 'Sister ...' I began, but her small hands gripped me so tightly that it hurt; she held on to me as a terrified child holds on to its mother.

" 'I don't know ... I don't know ...' And that's

all she could say. I couldn't get another word out
of her."

"And that's all you remember?" asked the
psychiatrist.

The nun nodded her head. That was all.

"Now I understand it," Mother Miriam Ruth
said softly. "That was the beginning. The night
of the conception. That's why she burned the
sheets."

"When was that?" asked Dr. Livingston.

"The twenty-third of January. On that night
one of our elder nuns passed away."

Remembering the tombstone, Martha asked,
"Sister Paul?"

"Yes." The mother superior looked a bit startled, but let it pass. "I have no recollection of
Agnes's activities on that night. I was needed in
the sick room, and that's where I spent the entire evening and night.

"Even though she was very old, the end came
unexpectedly for Sister Paul. Her passing was
peaceful, though, thank God. Father Martineau
arrived in time to give her extreme unction, and
the sisters gathered around her door after the
last rites, to say good-bye and to pray for her
soul. God grant all of us so good a death.

"The doctor had been there and had left, but
there was still much to be done to ease her final
suffering; she couldn't breathe well, and her fe-
ver rose high. So I was kept pretty busy.

"I do remember, though, that Agnes looked in.
I seem to see her face in the doorway, seem to

see that look of sorrow in her eyes. She loved the old woman; everybody was fond of Sister Paul, she was very pious and she had the touch of true holiness. But Sister Agnes spent as much time as she could with her, and I never objected. Why should I? Sister Paul was totally good, and Agnes seemed to be in need of that goodness. Agnes kept herself pretty much apart, out of shyness, perhaps, or perhaps from a sense of how different she was from the others. Sister Paul appeared to be her only friend.

"Yes, I seem to recall her face in that doorway, her sad eyes fixed on the dying nun. Father Martineau held the crucifix to Sister Paul's lips, for a last kiss. Now I remember something else. After she'd kissed the cross, Sister Paul turned her head a little and looked at Agnes. And she said something to her, or tried to, I'm not sure which. Whatever it was, I didn't hear it."

"Are you positive?" demanded Martha. "Try to think. Any clue at all!"

But the reverend mother just shook her head. "I'm not even sure it *was* a word. Maybe it was a last unspoken blessing, I don't know. Besides, what could it possibly have to do with what happened later? The old woman died that night!

"After that, I have no idea where Agnes might have gone or what she might have done. It never occurred to me to try to find out. I suppose that if you'd asked me about it the next day, I might have guessed that she'd gone to the chapel to pray for Sister Paul. Agnes often prayed by herself."

"So that was the night," breathed Martha. "The night she burned the sheets."

"It must have been," Mother Miriam Ruth replied wearily. "The dates fit."

"But how did she get out of the convent? Where did she go? How did she get back inside?"

"Believe me, I wish I knew."

Eight

It hardly came as a surprise to Dr. Livingston when Monsignor Tremblay summoned her to meet with him to discuss the case of Sister Agnes. She had been made aware from the beginning that the Church took a strong interest in its outcome; the defense attorney, Lyon, had been retained by the monsignor personally on behalf of the bishop. And she knew that every word spoken at this meeting would be reported back to the bishop, syllable by syllable. The bishop was a very important man in Montreal.

What surprised her was that they had waited this long. She had already been on the case three weeks, possibly two weeks longer than she might have taken to give a psychiatric evaluation in an ordinary case. She didn't have to sense the impatience that the religious authorities were feeling; it had already been expressed to her by Lyon. Now she was about to experience it firsthand.

As the bishop's right-hand man, with responsibility for the Berthierville convent, the monsignor took care of all the unpleasant and tedious tasks that the bishop was spared. I guess that includes me, thought Martha as she was shown into his study in the bishop's residence. Noticing with gratitude an ashtray on the large walnut desk, she was lighting a cigarette when the monsignor strode in, cassock flapping around his ankles.

He was a tall man, distinguished looking rather than handsome, and younger than Dr. Livingston had expected one in so responsible a position to be. She surmised—correctly—that he was intelligent and ambitious as well as hardworking. She could easily picture him in an archbishop's robes, and he wouldn't look too shabby dressed in cardinal's scarlet, either.

He greeted her politely, offering her coffee, which she declined.

"It's a beautiful day," said the monsignor, "and I hardly ever get a chance to stretch my legs out of doors. Would you object if we took a short walk while we talked?"

"Not at all."

The grounds surrounding the cathedral and the bishop's residence were extensive and well kept, neatly trimmed box hedges outlining the flower beds. Behind the cathedral, they were less manicured and preserved more of a rustic feeling. The two of them turned down the path leading to the less cultivated area, and the monsignor gave a sharp whistle. At once, the bishop's dog, a pedigreed and silky golden retriever, came bounding up to be walked, leash in mouth.

The monsignor knelt to fasten the leash to the dog's collar. "His Excellency wants me to express his gratitude to you for the special care you are taking with this case."

"Thank you," replied Martha, but she wasn't fooled. The words *special care* she translated to mean *taking your own sweet time,* and she was right.

"I've been told you don't recommend that Sister Agnes be returned to the convent."

"No," conceded the doctor cautiously.

"Well, you're probably right about that," remarked the prelate, and Martha's eyes widened in surprise. "But it certainly can't benefit Agnes to have this investigation continued for any length of time."

"I've never called it an investigation. Why do you?"

"Your mother was a resident of Saint Catherine's Home before you moved her." It was more a statement than a question.

Dr. Livingston was taken aback at this sudden change in the line of questioning. "What has that got to do with anything?"

"And you had a sister who died in a convent," continued the monsignor smoothly.

Martha felt indignation beginning to rise from the pit of her stomach. "Who told you this?" she demanded.

"Do you still go to church?"

Fighting to keep her anger from overpowering her reason, "What business is this of yours?" she asked him coldly.

"We just wonder if you can be very objective about this case." The prelate's coldness was a match for her own.

"Look, Father, just because I don't subscribe to all the beliefs—"

The priest cut her off, and now his voice was a shade less cutting. "It makes no difference to us what you believe, Doctor, but it makes all the difference to Agnes."

This wasn't fair; this wasn't what she had expected. She'd thought she'd have to account for what was taking her so long to make up her professional mind. She never thought she'd be put in the position of having to defend her faith, or rather, the lack of it.

"But I don't understand. Are you expecting me to just condemn her—"

"Someone's got to suffer for this, Doctor," the priest said in a low voice. "We must be merciful and quick."

Martha put one hand instinctively to her throat. Merciful and quick. Merciful. Merciful ... do they really think I'm not being merciful to Agnes? Will they take her case away from me? No, they mustn't! I can't let them! But, with a sick feeling, she acknowledged to herself that they had the power to do exactly that.

The empty room held no secrets anymore, unless the whitewashed walls could talk. If they could, what would they say? If walls had tongues as well as ears, would they accuse Martha Livingston of confusing Sister Agnes with Sister Marie? Was she attempting to pull Agnes away from this sterile religious life as she had not had the chance to pull her own sister away? Was she attempting to punish Mother Miriam Ruth for the sins of the mother superior who had made the judgment call that cost her sister's life?

Agnes is not my sister; Mother Miriam Ruth is who she is, and nobody else.

"The devil's daughter . . ." The old voice, dripping hate, intruded into the bare chamber and into Dr. Livingston's thoughts. Martha turned from the window to find Sister Marguerite standing in the doorway of Agnes's old room, her wrinkled face an angry mask.

"The devil's daughter, that's who she is. I've been watching. We were fine before *she* came. She brought the devil here." The old woman took a step or two into the room. "There was blood on her hand that night. I saw it," she hissed, her eyes twin burning coals in her white face.

"Agnes?"

"No!"

The breath caught in Dr. Livingston's throat. "Who? Mother?"

The old nun stepped closer, close enough for Martha to smell her dry, bitter, aged scent. In a voice that was near a whisper, she told the doctor, "There's more blood between the two of them than you could even guess."

"What are you talking about?" Martha demanded, breathless.

"Cherchez dans les archives du couvent," whispered the nun mysteriously.

"What?"

"Look in the convent records," Sister Marguerite repeated in English, with a twisted malicious smile. Then she turned rather quickly for an old woman and left the room.

It took the psychiatrist a moment for what the nun had told her to sink in. She hurried to the door, but Sister Marguerite was already halfway down the long corridor.

"Sister! Sister!" called Martha after her, but Sister Marguerite didn't turn or even look back.

Look in the convent records. Sister Marguerite's words seemed to hang in the air, just out of Dr. Livingston's reach.

The convent stable was not to be confused with the barn. The barn had been built at the same time as the convent itself, in a more prosperous century, when the unmarriageable daughters of the middle class brought a marriage dowry with them into religious life. It had been built for a herd, which was reduced now to one solitary cow. These days the barn was completely unoccupied and almost never put to use.

The stable, on the other hand, was a far humbler and very much smaller structure; as such, it was in daily use. Their one cow had freshened, and it was the stable where she was milked every day.

Milking was a chore that Sister Agnes loved. The warmth of the stable, the sweet breath of the cow, the solidity of her flanks and the patient way she stood over the pail—all of these gave Agnes a sense of security and permanence. Cows were such peaceful animals, surely God must possess their souls above those of other dumb creatures.

She milked well, the white liquid pressed out between her long fingers, the udder slick with the balm they used to prevent chafing. The pail filled up quickly. If she had been alone, Sister Agnes would have pressed her cheek against the warm body of the cow, to feel the life within her. But she wasn't alone. Dr. Livingston was with her; it seemed to Agnes that Dr. Livingston was always with her these days. Always smoking those cigarettes, always asking her those questions, the questions that poked and probed at her, making her angry when anger was a mortal sin. It would never occur to Agnes that the questions were designed to anger her, to release her true emotions from their hiding place deep within her spirit.

Sister Marguerite had told her why the doctor came here all the time—to inform the police that she was crazy, or maybe that she wasn't crazy, so that she would have to stand trial for manslaughter, go into the courtroom in front of everybody. Agnes knew that Sister Marguerite hated her and was jealous of her.

Nevertheless, she believed the old nun and was beginning to understand what the psychiatrist wanted of her.

It was the first time that Agnes had ever had a person all to herself. Reverend Mother was always so busy with the others. Her own mother hadn't had time for her. Sister Paul had loved her, but she died. Father Martineau loved everybody equally. But Dr. Livingston concentrated only on her.

Why did it have to be Dr. Livingston, Agnes thought. Why can't she leave me alone? Why does she always hound me with those questions that always make me commit a sin?

"Sister Marguerite says I'm sick. I know that you think I'm sick. I'm not sick!"

"But you're troubled, aren't you?" asked the doctor.

The milk pail was full. Agnes set it out of reach of the cow's hooves and tail and stood up from the stool, shaking out her habit. "That's because you keep reminding me. If you go away, then I'll forget!"

"And you're unhappy," prompted the psychiatrist.

Picking up the milk pail, Agnes started for the door. "Everybody's unhappy! You're unhappy, aren't you?"

"Agnes . . ."

"Answer me! You never answer me!" the girl shouted angrily.

"Sometimes, yes," Martha conceded.

It was cold just inside the stable door, and the breath of the two women curled like puffs of smoke in the air.

"Only you think you're lucky because you didn't have a mother who said things to you and did things that weren't always nice, but that was because of me! Because I was bad, not her!" Agnes's face was pink with the effort to make the doctor understand.

"What did you do?"

"I'm always bad!" the girl cried.

Martha bore down relentlessly. "What did you do!"

With a convulsion that seemed to tear her apart, Agnes flung the words out of her deepest being. "I *breathe!*"

She slammed the milk pail to the stable floor. The white fluid sloshed out of the top, and the pail itself tilted precariously, almost ready to tip over. Throwing herself to the ground, Agnes grabbed for the pail. A storm of weeping overtook her, and she began to cry in great, shuddering sobs.

Martha knelt beside her in the odorous straw. The girl's defenses had been devastated by a ferocious force. Now she must finish what she'd begun. She must reach all the way down, no matter how painful, and bring up the hurt. Bring it up and look at it, so that it could begin to heal. "What did your mother do to you?" she insisted.

But Sister Agnes only shook her head, unable to speak through the weeping, refusing to give voice to the terrible words.

"If you can't tell me, shake your head yes or no," pressed the doctor. "Did she hit you?"

Agnes shook her head no.

"Did she make you do something you didn't want to do?"

The cowled head nodded a faint yes.

"Did it make you uncomfortable to do this?"

Again, a yes.

"Did it embarrass you?"

Yes. It was apparent that a great struggle was going on inside the girl; the strain on her face attested to it.

"Did it hurt you?"

Yes. The strain intensified into fear, mirrored in the dark pupils of Agnes's eyes.

"What did she make you do?"

"No," said the girl, refusing to meet Martha's eyes.

"You can tell me," insisted Martha.

"I can't." A cry from the heart, delivered in a hoarse whisper.

"She's dead, isn't she?" Martha said.

"Yes."

"She can't hurt you anymore."

The girl raised her head and looked the doctor in the face. "She can," she whispered.

"How?"

"She watches. She listens." There was no mistaking the real fear on that tearstained face.

"Agnes, I don't believe that," said the psychiatrist evenly. "Tell me. I'll protect you from her."

The girl's eyes searched Martha's, looking for assurance. She seemed to find it, for she tried to talk. "She . . ."

"Yes?" prompted Dr. Livingston.

Agnes was taking deep, ragged breaths, gulping for air. Her words came out unevenly, in a stammer of fear, as she relived what she had spent years trying to forget. "She . . . makes me . . . take off my clothes . . . and then . . ."

"Yes?"

"She makes . . . fun of me . . ."

"She tells you you're ugly?" Martha's voice was very gentle.

"Yes."

"And stupid."

"Yes."

"And that you're a mistake."

A look of great suffering passed over the girl's face, and the features contorted in pain. "She says . . . my whole body . . . is a mistake . . ."

"Why?" The psychiatrist drew deeply on her cigarette, narrowing her eyes against the smoke.

"Because she says . . . if I don't watch out . . . I'll have a baby."

"How does she know that?"

"Her headaches."

"Oh, yes." The famous headaches through which the angel would speak to Mummy.

Now the girl's voice dropped to a whisper, and she turned her face away so that the doctor couldn't see her eyes. She had gone too far to turn back, but she was at the deepest place of all, where the hurt was too painful to bear.

"And then . . . she touches me . . ."

"Where?" demanded Martha. She had to bend closer to hear the girl's next words.

"Down there . . . with her cigarette."

Stunned, Dr. Livingston gasped and drew back. Then she became conscious of the cigarette she held in her hand, the cigarette that had so frightened Agnes the last time they'd met. Instantly, she ground it out on the stony earth. Her mind was shaking from the girl's words. In her years of experience as a psychiatrist, she'd heard many horror stories, but nothing to match Sister Agnes's.

The young nun was talking again, but her voice was totally different. No longer ragged, it was that of a little girl, a frightened little girl.

"Please, Mummy, don't touch me like that. I'll be good. I won't be your bad baby anymore."

A great sadness took possession of Martha, mingled with a fierce determination to heal this pitiful child. She took Agnes into her arms, turning her so that she could look into the girl's face.

"Agnes, dear, I want you to do something. I want you to pretend that I'm your mother. Only this time, I want you to tell me what you're feeling. All right?"

Sister Agnes drew back, shaking her head. "I'm afraid."

With gentle hands, Martha cupped the girl's face. "Please. I want to help you. Let me help you."

For the first time, Sister Agnes looked closely into Martha Livingston's face, at the resolute mouth, the honesty of the blue eyes, the sympathy in the woman's expression. For the first time, Sister Agnes extended her fragile trust.

"All right," she whispered.

"Good." She pushed the girl away and, becoming Agnes's mother, assumed a different facial expression. Disapproving, angry. "Agnes, you're ugly. What do you say?"

Confused, the girl answered, "I don't know."

"Of course you do. Agnes, you're ugly." When the girl didn't answer, she pushed harder. "What do you say?"

"No, I'm not!" Agnes cried out.

It was the first step, a giant one. Martha smiled to herself. "Are you pretty?" she demanded.

"Yes!"

"Agnes, you're stupid." The mother again.

"No, I'm not," quavered Agnes, still unsure.

"Are you intelligent?"

"Yes, I am."

"Agnes, you're a mistake."

Now the long-suppressed denial came bursting forth. "I'm not a mistake! I'm here, aren't I?

How can I be a mistake when I'm really here? God doesn't make mistakes! You're a mistake! I wish you were dead!" Tears spilled out of her eyes and down her cheeks as she broke away and ran out of the stable into the cold.

"Agnes!" called Dr. Livingston after her. She broke into a run, catching up with the girl and taking her into her arms. Like a mother, a loving mother, she held Agnes tightly, rocking her and soothing her, whispering reassurances.

"It's all right. It's all right," she shushed her. "Agnes, I love you. It's all right."

The girl pulled back a little to look into the woman's face.

"Do you really love me?" she pleaded. "Or are you just saying that?"

"I really love you," whispered Martha. It's true, she thought in amazement. I really do love her.

"As much as Mother Miriam Ruth loves me?"

"As much," said the rational psychiatrist, "as God loves you."

Nine

There was a century and a half of history in the basement record room, and most of it was piled to the ceiling in no particular order. Dark, cluttered with file boxes, bins, cartons, and some ancient oak filing cabinets, the convent archives represented an impenetrable labyrinth to the uninitiated. It was Sister David Marie's domain, and hardly anybody ever disturbed her in the possession of it. Once filed away safely, records were rarely taken out again.

Dr. Livingston hadn't the smallest idea where to begin. She could only surmise that, Agnes's records being recent, not ancient history, they might be somewhat less inaccessible than earlier records. So she opened the file drawer nearest to her and began searching through it.

She wasn't supposed to be here, and she knew it. She was trespassing, without permission and without authority. But Sister Marguerite's words echoed in her head. "Look in the convent's records." Something was here that she was supposed to know, locked away where she wasn't meant to find it.

A sound behind her made Martha jump. She turned to find Sister David Marie watching her from the doorway, baffled. The sister was in sole charge of this archive, and she was astonished to find her domain intruded upon, especially by an outsider.

"Good evening, Sister. I need some biographical data on Sister Agnes. Mother said that I'd find it here," lied Martha through her teeth.

She held her breath in suspense while Sister David Marie thought it over.

Even though nuns have little experience of lying, it occurred to the sister that a secular psychiatrist might just be capable of taking the reverend mother's name in vain. Still, she had no authority to question the doctor. So Sister David Marie went dutifully over to the correct cabinet and lifted a file folder out of the middle drawer, placing it on top of the oak cabinet so that the doctor could read it more easily.

"Thank you," Martha said uncomfortably. She waited until she saw Sister David Marie leave the basement room. It never occurred to her that the nun might go straight to the mother superior with a report. Little did Martha really know of the way of convents.

Now she turned all her attention to the folder. The file was a slim one, some biographical and medical information and little else. Dr. Livingston saw nothing in the folder to warrant Sister Marguerite's mysterious advice. She tried to recall the nun's exact words.

"There's more blood between the two of them than you could even guess."

Between the two of them. The two of them.

Opening the same drawer from which Sister David Marie had pulled Agnes's file, Martha flipped rapidly through the other files until she found the one she wanted. The name on the folder: Miriam Ruth. She pulled it out and, opening it, began to read.

Here, too, the information was of the scantiest and most ordinary kind. But there was something . . .

"Born:" the sheet of paper read, "Anna Marie Burchetti." Mother Miriam Ruth had been Anna Marie Burchetti. And in Sister Agnes's folder . . . "Mother: Mary Eugene Burchetti." Another piece of the puzzle fell into place. *More blood between them* . . . She quickly stuffed both folders back into their drawer. Armed with this bit of information, perhaps the psychiatrist could force the mother superior's full cooperation now.

Dr. Livingston had started up the stairs from the basement when she was confronted by Mother Miriam Ruth on her way down.

"You lied to me!" she growled at the mother superior.

"About what?"

"Your niece!" Mother Miriam Ruth stiffened and a small gasp escaped her lips.

For a moment, the two women just glared at each other, then the mother superior dropped her eyes. "I didn't tell you because I didn't think it was important." She turned and started back up the stairs with the doctor behind her.

"No, it just makes you doubly responsible, doesn't it?" Martha followed the nun down the long hallway toward her office. The convent was very quiet; the sisters had already retired for the night. As she passed down the hall, Mother Miriam Ruth snapped off the few electric lights that were allowed for illumination; the Little Sisters of Mary Magdalene were closing down for the night.

"I never saw Agnes until she set foot in this convent!" The mother superior lowered her voice. Even though the nuns were all in their rooms on the third floor, sound travels. "My sister ran away from home. We lost touch with her. When my husband died and I came here, she wrote to me and asked me to watch over Agnes in case anything happened."

They had reached Mother Miriam Ruth's office now, but she didn't go in. Instead, she reached around the doorframe and snapped off the light. Now the convent was in almost total darkness. One foyer light was burning still, and the mother superior headed in that direction, making it very plain that she was ushering the doctor to the front door; it was time for Martha to leave.

But Martha wasn't ready to go yet. "And Agnes's father?" she prompted.

Mother Miriam Ruth shrugged. "Could have been any one of a dozen men from what my sister told me. She was afraid that Agnes would follow in her footsteps. She did everything to prevent that."

"By keeping her home from school," Martha said with sarcasm.

"Yes."

"And listening to angels."

The mother superior ignored that and unbolted the front door. "She drank too much. That's what killed her."

"Do you know what she did to Agnes?" asked Dr. Livingston with great emphasis on every syllable.

The nun refused to meet her eyes. Instead she opened the door for the doctor. "I don't think I care to know," she said evenly.

"She molested her," Martha said distinctly.

A stunned silence followed in which tears sprang to Mother Miriam Ruth's eyes. Instinctively, her hands reached up and clasped the crucifix she wore.

"Oh, dear Jesus," she whispered.

"There *is* more here than meets the eye, isn't there?" demanded the doctor. "Lots of dirty little secrets." Her lips twisted in scorn.

"Had I known what Agnes was suffering—"

But Martha wouldn't let her continue. "Why didn't you?" she challenged. "My God, you knew she was keeping the child from school. You knew she was an alcoholic."

The mother superior kept shaking her head, her eyes dark with sorrow. "I knew that after the fact—"

But Martha was like some avenging angel with a sword. Her blue eyes flashed in anger. "Why didn't you do anything to stop her?" she demanded.

"I didn't know! I didn't know!" Tears coursed down the older woman's face, blurring the features. "And that's no answer, is it?" She looked pleadingly at Martha, who was made of stone.

"No. That's no answer." As she got into her car, Martha heard the heavy front door close after her, heard the bolt slam. No answer at all.

What then had she accomplished, besides making the mother superior feel guilty? Oddly, Martha didn't feel good about that, not as good as she'd expected to feel. She'd been waiting to give a mother superior one in the eye ever since Marie's death, and that was a long time ago. Now that she had, she found it a hollow victory.

On the way back from Berthierville, she went over and over in her mind what Agnes had told her, memorizing it for her notebook later. A classic case of child abuse. An alcoholic mother whose sexuality was ever at war with her religious upbringing. Who got drunk, had headaches, and talked to angels. A "mistake"—an unwanted child punished for the parent's sins. A sense of physical shame instilled in the child early and reinforced by frequent brutal behavior; deprivation of normal childish occupations, like school and playmates; an enforced isolation—the pattern was clear. It would be miraculous if Agnes *hadn't* grown up hearing voices.

But something was still missing. The more she saw the girl, the more unreal the idea of her strangling a newborn seemed to Martha. She kept trying to picture it in her mind, but she always failed. The case appeared to be more mysterious than ever. If Dr. Livingston thought before this that Mother Miriam Ruth had reason to protect her nun, how much more reason did she have as her aunt!

As she drove back to Montreal, she went over the missing pieces of the puzzle. Even assuming that Sister Agnes was guilty as charged, how the hell did she get out of the convent to meet him? Mother Miriam Ruth's security system was tighter than the Bank of Canada's. The Bank of Canada might have the latest in protective devices, but the Little Sisters of Mary Magdalen had Sister Marguerite. If Agnes did get out, how many times did she have to get out before she became pregnant?

If she didn't get out, how the hell did he get in?

And who the hell was he?

She was pregnant. How likely was it that, loose

habit or not, she managed to conceal it from everybody else in the convent, including a mother superior who'd twice given birth herself? What about her fear and confusion? Could the same girl who had a hysterical conniption over blood on her sheets remain calm for nine months while her body was going through such heavy changes? What about morning sickness?

And when the labor began, what did Sister Agnes do? How long does it take for a first labor, hours and hours? Did she really believe for hours and hours that it was something she ate? When the cramps became contractions and the contractions swelled to waves of agony, what did Sister Agnes do? How did she bear it when she saw the blood? There was so very much blood.

And Mother Miriam Ruth. The night the infant was probably conceived, she was attending Sister Paul on her deathbed. But where the hell was she nine months later, on the night the baby was born? What was her excuse then?

No. Too damn many missing pieces. And too many pieces that didn't fit at all, that seemed to belong to a different puzzle entirely.

Innocent or guilty? Innocent or guilty? The question kept nagging at Martha, though she knew she was not authorized to be asking it.

The last few weeks had drained her. In addition to her visits to the convent and her confrontations with Agnes and her mother superior, Martha was also juggling her private practice and trying to keep the Roman Catholic Church off her back. Her social life no longer existed, and her love life had come down to sharing her pillow with her cat. And the cat snored.

What she really needed was about fourteen hours of uninterrupted sleep. A big snifter of Napoleon brandy, a long, steaming bath, and a saucer of hot milk shared with Mitzi ought to do it. Nevertheless, when she reached the city, she found herself driving not to Westmount, where she lived, but downtown to the central police station, where Richard Langevin worked. She hoped he was on duty tonight; it had been several days since she'd spoken to him.

He was there, wearily grilling a little teenage hooker, who sat sobbing in fear and humiliation. This was her first arrest, and she had visions of a century at hard labor in some Devil's Island of a prison.

"Pourquoi me mentis-tu, Madeleine?" demanded the detective. *"Pourquoi me dis-tu que tu ne le connais pas? T'as quel age?"*

"Dix-huit," the girl hiccuped.

Langevin looked at her skeptically. If she was eighteen, then he was eighteen. *"Quel age?"* he growled one more time.

The girl dropped her eyes. *"J'ai seize ans."* She admitted to sixteen. *"Mais je vais avoir dix-sept ans le mois prochain."*

"Bonne anniversaire," remarked Langevin sarcastically, then looked up to find Dr. Livingston watching him from the doorway of his office.

"Marty! What are you doing here?"

"Richard, there's got to be something missing," Martha began without preamble.

"I gave you the pictures, Marty, what else do you want?"

"Something they might have overlooked."

Langevin's rugged face looked surprised, something it rarely did, considering the profession he was in. "What? You think the girl's innocent?"

Martha shook her head. "I don't know," she confessed.

"You've got to be crazy." The detective scowled.

"Look, Richard . . ."

"What's gotten into you?" he demanded. "You've seen the report. It's a cut-and-dried case."

But Martha persisted. "Was there anything *not* in the report that should have been?"

"You're too involved!" exploded Langevin. "Look at you, Marty! My God! Why don't you turn this case over to someone else."

She met his explosion with silence, the silence of stubbornness. She knew that he was concerned only for her, and that he was right. She was too deeply involved. As for turning the case over to another psychiatrist, that was clearly impossible. She had come too far to go back now, no matter what the bishop or the police might have to say. She had to see it through. There was more at stake here than a young nun going to prison or not. As far as Martha could see, Agnes was already in prison, had been in prison all her short life. Dr. Livingston was the only person capable of setting her free.

Martha's silence defeated Richard as no words of hers ever could. He sighed, capitulating, then got up from his chair, went over, and wrapped his arms around her.

"Okay. I'll ask around, see what I come up with. In the meantime, go home, for Christ's sake. Get some sleep. I'll call you later."

He kissed her lightly, but Marty was too tired to respond. She accepted his kiss and his words with a weary smile and a nod.

Langevin watched her go. When she turned the corner of the corridor and could no longer be seen, he turned his attention back to the little sixteen-year-old prostitute.

"Je n'ai pas fini avec toi. Bon! On recommence par le début."

I'm not finished with you. Let's go back and start all over, from the beginning . . . Now, why did you say you didn't know the guy . . .

Martha almost had to drag herself out of her car and into her apartment building. Exhaustion deep in her bones, she took the thick pile of mail out of the mailbox and rang for the elevator. She was too tired even to thumb through the envelopes to see if there was anything interesting or even urgent. Tomorrow, maybe. Or the next day.

Opening her door, Martha threw the mail onto the hall table that already held a large stack of unopened envelopes and turned on her television set to catch the eleven o'clock English-language news. She hadn't read a paper in several days and had no idea what was happening in the rest of the world.

But the newsman was reporting on the war between Iran and Iraq, and Martha couldn't keep her mind on what he was saying. The headlines seemed to come from a distant planet in another century. With Mitzi mewing for attention at her heels, Martha went into the kitchen and poured them both some milk. The only difference was that she took a sleeping pill with hers.

"There is still no progress being made toward the trial of the young nun accused of manslaughter and the death of her newborn infant," said the newscaster, riveting Martha's attention to the television set.

"Some of the media are charging the Catholic Church with deliberately dragging its feet in the case. Sister Agnes, of the Little Sisters of Mary Magdalene, a cloistered order near Berthierville, was indicted for manslaughter on the fourteenth of this month, but a trial date has not been set. The Montreal *Gazette,* in an article this morning, has accused the Church of, and we quote, 'Ostrich mentality, hoping that the case will just disappear.' Monsignor Tremblay, assistant to the bishop in charge of the Berthierville area, has this to say . . ."

The face of the monsignor, distinguished and serious, appeared on the screen. "In no way is the Church trying to run away from this incident," he began gravely, "but we wish to impress upon the public that this is a rare and tragic occurrence for all of us. I assure you that as soon as certain legal procedures are accomplished, a trial date will be set."

The monsignor's image was replaced by some file footage of the convent behind its walls, and the newscaster's voice-over reported, "Until that time, Sister Agnes is being kept in seclusion in the Berthierville convent. Elsewhere in the news today . . ."

Snapping off the TV, Martha walked into the bathroom and turned the taps on in the tub. She knew she had better get a bath going before the sleeping pill began to take action, or they'd find her floating face down in three inches of water tomorrow. The tub was filling nicely when Martha remembered her telephone messages. Half naked, she went back to turn on her answering machine, setting the volume knob at the highest so that she could hear over the sound of the running water.

"Hi, Marty. It's Helen. Mrs. Davenport called and was very upset that you missed her appointment. She wants you to call her at home: nine-four-three-eight-four-seven-seven. If you want my opinion, it'll wait until tomorrow. Oh, and a couple of reporters have been trying to get hold of you about Sister Agnes. They seemed persistent and they may try to reach you at home. I didn't give them your number."

Click.

"Dr. Livingston, this is Mrs. Davenport." The voice sounded really annoyed. "Would you please call me at home? I would appreciate talking to you."

Click.

Martha tested the water with her big toe, then added a little more cold.

"Hi, Marty. I've been trying to call you for days." Tom's voice, anxious and insecure. "Is anything wrong? I'd love to see you soon."

Click.

She shook her head, half pleased, half exasperated. Would she ever have a normal social life again? I doubt it. I'm too damn tired, she thought. Filling the sink, Martha dropped in her panty hose and bra to rinse while she bathed. She caught a glimpse of herself in the medicine-cabinet mirror, and the look of strain around her eyes and mouth caught her by surprise. I look like ten pounds of crap in a five-pound sack, she thought, horrified. Got to get some rest, I can't go on like this. As a scientist, she was aware of the toll that fatigue takes on the brain, especially on judgment.

"Hello, Dr. Livingston," said a voice with a French accent. "My name is Charlie Sexton, and I'm doing a Sunday article on Sister Agnes for the Montreal *Gazette*. I would appreciate it if you would give me a call."

Click.

Wearily, Martha eased herself into the tub, letting her tired body sink into the steaming water. Sorry, Charlie. She reached for her cigarettes, which were resting handily on the top of the toilet.

"Hi, Marty, Helen again. Your court appearance for the shoplifting case has been moved to Monday. And the Crown attorney's office called. There's an exhibitionist coming up for trial in a couple of weeks. They want you to talk to him. Can I come along? Bye."

Click.

The heat of the water combined with the sleeping pill to lull her, dulling her senses. In a minute or two she'd have to climb out of here . . . just roll into bed wrapped in a towel . . .

"Hi, Marty, this is Langevin. I just talked with Detective Crowley, who was at the convent. She said there was something that bothered her . . ."

She was almost half asleep now. God, it felt good! Whatever Langevin wanted, it could wait until tomorrow . . .

Langevin? And he said something about the convent, and a detective? Suddenly, Martha was wide-awake and grabbing for a towel, tossing her unlit cigarette into the toilet, running to the machine to rewind the last message. As she heard Richard's voice, her every nerve end was standing at attention.

"Hi, Marty, this is Langevin. I just talked with Detective Crowley, who was at the convent. She said there was one thing that bothered her that didn't make it into the report. The wastepaper basket. The one in Agnes's room. None of the other nuns had one."

Click.

The wastepaper basket. She grabbed up another cigarette and lit it, smoking furiously while her mind raced. The wastepaper basket. It was important; she was convinced of it. And there was something more ... something she couldn't remember ... something about a wastepaper basket, not Agnes's ... but tied in somehow with Agnes's ... damn! it eluded her.

I won't sleep until I remember.

Then the sleeping pill caught up with her, and she barely had time to make it to the bed, where she dreamed that a wastepaper basket streaming blood had grown tiny little feet and was coming in her direction, not quickly, but one sure step at a time.

Ten

Except for the pigeons, the barn appeared to be deserted. The cow was stabled for the night, the stalls empty. The pigeons had taken dominion over the vast stone building. There were literally hundreds of them, nesting, cooing, rustling their feathers as they settled down for the night. The last rays of the sun, coming in through the hayloft windows, turned their iridescent feathers to rainbows. Dr. Livingston's entrance caused panic in their ranks; they took wing, fluttered a few seconds, then, perceiving no real threat, settled down into their nests again.

But there was somebody in the barn. Somebody Martha had come to find.

Through the sound of their murmured coos, Martha heard the soft whisper of the rosary's prayers, the faint click of beads. She followed the sound. Mother Miriam Ruth was on her knees before the window, saying her rosary in the last dying light of the day. At the sound of feet, the mother superior turned, hardly believing that anybody would dare to intrude upon her solitary prayers. This place was a kind of private chapel of hers; she came here for a rare moment of privacy.

"I've gotten the court's permission to hypnotize her," said the doctor without ceremony.

"And *my* permission?" The nun got to her feet, a frown drawing a thick vertical line between her dark brows.

"I'd like yours, too," Martha answered.

"Well, we'll see about that," said Mother Miriam Ruth as she brushed past the psychiatrist.

"You'll deny it?" asked the doctor anxiously.

"I haven't decided yet."

"This woman's health is at stake!" Martha cried.

"Her spiritual health."

"I don't give a damn about her spiritual health!" Blue sparks flashed from the psychiatrist's eyes.

"I know you don't," retorted the mother superior a little smugly.

"'Sentence her and be done with it,' that's what you're saying, isn't it?" Martha cried passionately. "Well, I can't do that yet."

"What I'm saying," Mother Miriam Ruth began persuasively, "is that you have a beautifully simple woman—"

"An unhappy woman," interrupted the doctor.

"She is happy with us!" cried the nun strongly. "And she could go on being happy if she were left alone."

"Then why did you call the police in the first place?" argued Martha. "Why didn't you just throw the baby in the incinerator and be done with it?"

"Because I am a moral person!" shouted Mother Miruam Ruth.

"Bullshit!"

"Bullshit yourself!"

At the sound of the women's voices raised in a quarrel, the pigeons stirred uneasily and rustled their wings, ready to fly at the next alarm.

Dr. Livingston made an effort to calm herself. A shouting match would get neither of them anywhere. In a much quieter voice, she said, "The Catholic Church doesn't have a corner on morality, Mother."

"Who said anything about the Catholic Church?" The mother superior toned down her voice as well.

"You just said that you—"

"What the hell does the Catholic Church have to do with you?" demanded Mother Miriam Ruth suddenly.

"Nothing," Martha said evasively, not meeting the other woman's eyes.

"What have we done to hurt you? And don't deny it. I can smell an ex-Catholic a mile away. What did we do? Burn a few heretics? Sell some

indulgences? That was in the days when the
Church was a ruling body. We let governments
do those things today. So tell me," she challenged Martha. "What did we do to *you*? You
wanted to neck in the backseat of a car when you
were fifteen, and you couldn't because it was a
sin, so instead of questioning that one little rule—"

"It wasn't sex!" protested Martha, the color
rising in her face betraying her emotion. "It was a
lot of things, but it wasn't sex! When I was in
the first grade, my best friend was run over on
her way to school. The nun said she died because
she hadn't said her morning prayers."

"Stupid woman," commented Mother Miriam
Ruth.

"Yeah."

"That's all?"

"That's all!" yelled Martha. "That's enough!"
She was a *beautiful* little girl—"

"What's that got to do with it?"

"I wasn't! She was the pretty one and she
died! Why not me? I never said my morning
prayers. And I was ugly! I was scrawny, I had
big buckteeth, freckles all over my face . . . Sister
Mary Cletus used to call me Polka-Dot Livingston." Martha stopped, aware that she had betrayed more of herself than she had intended.

Mother Miriam Ruth recognized the pain behind the doctor's words. But she wasn't willing
to let go yet, not when she'd found an advantage.
Softly she said, "So you left the Church because
you had freckles?"

"No!" cried Martha, then she saw the mother superior's raised eyebrow and one-sided smile. "Yeah . . . I left the Church because I had freckles. And guess what?"

"What?"

"That's also why I hate nuns!"

At the sound of both women's voices raised in shouts of laughter, the pigeons rose en masse from the rafters, flying in circles under the barn roof, swooping and diving and fluttering their wings in panic.

"I feel like a statue in the park," joked Martha. "Let's get the hell out of here."

The anger between the two was now dissipated by their laughter, just as a fresh wind sends clouds scattering before it, letting the sun's rays through to warm the earth. For the first time, they seemed to see each other as women, not symbols of religious and secular authorities. They looked at each other with unprejudiced eyes and realized how much they had in common, and how in other circumstances they might have become good friends. Now, for the first time, they might even be able to talk together about Sister Agnes without the barriers of resentment and misunderstanding that had held them apart.

Quitting the barn, they walked into the convent gardens. The last light of day was about to leave the sky, and it was getting colder, but neither woman wanted to break away from the other. There was still so much to be said!

A small round gazebo of wood and stone sat in the center of the gardens, a relic of former and grander times. These days it was never in use, except for the occasional field-mouse family that nested there undisturbed in the summer. There was a bench running all the way around the interior. Dr. Livingston and the mother superior sat down side by side, for a few minutes not saying anything but listening to the sounds that signal the oncoming of night in the country. Martha lit a cigarette and inhaled deeply, still somewhat drained. She was unused to quarreling, taking always the approach of reason.

Mother Miriam Ruth gazed off into the encroaching evening. "When I was a child," she began softly, half to herself, "I used to hear my guardian angel. She sang to me until I was six years old. That's when I stopped listening and my angel stopped singing, but I remember that voice. A few years ago, I looked at myself one day and saw a nun who was certain of nothing. Not even of heaven. Not even of God. And then, one evening, I saw Agnes standing at her window, singing. And all my doubts about God and myself vanished in that one moment. I recognized the voice." She turned to look at the psychiatrist in the fading light.

"Don't take it away from me again, Dr. Livingston," she pleaded. "Those years after six were very bleak."

Martha inhaled deeply. Inside, she struggled to understand a woman like Mother Miriam Ruth.

Here was somebody who had effectively lived two lives, each the opposite of the other. She had been out in the world, married, borne two daughters. Unsuccessful at marriage and motherhood, or so she claimed, but who really knows what success is? And all the while, she longed for a totally different kind of life—a life of celibacy, fasting, prayer, and self-denial. Then, as soon as widowhood set her free, she had run to that other life and made such a success of it that here she was now, mother superior of a convent. What a paradox! But what strength of purpose!

Even so, this same woman, strong and commanding, was still attached to that little girl who lives inside of her, who heard a guardian angel singing in a simpler time. A woman for whom a young nun has come to symbolize that simplicity and innocence. Innocence. When Mother Miriam Ruth heard Sister Agnes singing, she recaptured that bygone innocence. No wonder she didn't want to let Agnes go! The girl stood between the mother superior and the loss of her immortal soul!

"My sister died in a convent," said Martha quietly. "And it's her voice I hear."

Ah, so that's where Martha Livingston's fear and resentment comes from. Little wonder, the nun thought, and leaned over to touch the doctor gently on her arm. Martha took another cigarette from her purse and lit chain style from the butt of the one she was smoking.

"Does my smoking bother you?" asked Martha, suddenly concerned.

"No, it only reminds me." The mother superior smiled.

Martha held out the pack. "Would you like one?" she offered.

Mother Miriam Ruth put up her hand to ward off the temptation, but her eyes remained glued to the package. It was a real struggle, and a losing one. "I'd love one," she admitted finally, reaching for the pack. Laughing, Martha lit one up and handed it over. The nun took a deep drag and broke into a fit of coughing.

"I'm out of practice," she gasped. But she took another puff.

"Do you think"—the doctor smiled wickedly—"that the saints would have smoked if tobacco had been popular back then?"

"Undoubtedly." The nun nodded. "Not the ascetics, of course. But . . . well . . . Saint Thomas More."

"Long, thin, and unfiltered." Martha grinned.

Mother Miriam Ruth mulled it over for a moment. "Saint Ignatius, I think, would smoke cigars and then stub them out on the soles of his feet."

They both found the game extremely funny, like mischievous children. Warming to the topic, the mother superior continued judiciously, "And, of course, all the apostles . . ."

"Hand rolled," put in the doctor, giggling.

"And even Christ would partake socially."

"Saint Peter?" asked Martha.

"A pipe," Mother Miriam Ruth answered decisively. For some reason, both of them found this hilarious, and they choked on their laughter, tears coming to their eyes. They were like a pair of naughty parochial-school kids, whispering blasphemies at recess and waiting for God to strike one or the other of them dead. The game was thrilling, not only because it was so silly but because it was probably forbidden.

"Mary Magdalene?" aked Mother Miriam Ruth, granting Martha a turn.

" 'You've come a long way, baby.' " This broke them up totally, and their rib cages began to ache from so much laughing.

"Saint Joan . . ." gasped the nun, "Saint Joan would . . . chew tobacco!"

This was the paralyzer, absolutely the cherry on the whipped cream on the cake. They doubled over, trying to get their breath, until the tears rolled over their cheeks and they could laugh no more.

It was quite dark now, the sun had long set, but it was still too early for the moon. And it was cold. The wind had risen, and the fallen leaves whirled around their legs. By unspoken agreement, the nun and the psychiatrist stood up and brushed off their clothing.

"And what, do you suppose, are today's saints smoking?" asked Martha lightly.

Mother Miriam Ruth smiled at her. "Oh, there are no saints today. Good people, yes. But extraordinarily good people? I'm afraid those we are sorely lacking."

"Do you believe they ever existed?"

"Yes, I do," replied the mother superior gravely.

"Would you like to become one?" Ever the scientist, always the prober.

The black brows rose again, almost to the line of the wimple. "To *become*?" she asked quietly. "One is born a saint. Only no one is born a saint today. We're too ... complicated." There was genuine sorrow in Mother Miriam Ruth's voice.

"You can try, can't you?" Martha was taking this as seriously as the mother superior. "To be good?"

"Oh, yes, but goodness has very little to do with sainthood. Not all of the saints were good. In fact, most of them were a little crazy. But they were still attached to God, left in His hands at birth." She spoke very softly, but her eyes shone, even in the surrounding darkness.

Martha had a sudden unasked-for vision of those saints of centuries ago, childlike, crazy, attached to the deity. Not, perhaps, unlike Sister Agnes. She sighed.

Mother Miriam Ruth put her cigarette out carefully and left the gazebo, striding quickly across the garden toward the convent. Her face was very sad. "No more," she murmured. "We're born, we live, we die." She stopped and waited for Dr. Livingston to catch up with her. "There's no *room* for miracles anymore. But oh, my dear," she whispered, "how I miss the miracles!"

Now they walked slowly together, side by side. Mother Miriam Ruth took Dr. Livingston's arm.

"Do you believe Agnes is still attached to God?" the doctor asked.

"If you doubt it, listen to her singing."

"I'd like to begin," said Martha quietly.

"Begin what?"

"The hypnotism. Do you still disapprove?"

The nun shot her a quizzical glance. "Will it stop you if I do?"

"No." Martha smiled.

"No, I didn't think so. May I be present?" asked Mother Miriam Ruth.

"Of course."

"Then let's begin."

Eleven

The room was high up, directly under the convent roof, far removed from the bedrooms of the
sleeping nuns. It was windowless, therefore
womblike. During the day, light entered it through
a skylight, but when the darkness came, unless
the moon was very bright, the room had to be lit
by a candle. This room had not been used since
the old days when the convent was filled to ca-
pacity and the novices had to be put into the
top-floor chambers. There was no longer any furniture in it, only the crucifix on the wall. It was
here they brought Agnes, still in her white linen
nightgown.

She came reluctantly, and only after Mother
Miriam Ruth had taken her in her arms to reas-
sure her for several minutes. Even then she was

afraid, and the sight of the empty room, so like a prison cell in its spareness and remoteness, made her pull back from the mother superior's restraining arm and turn to run.

"No, Agnes, you have to stay. Nothing is going to hurt you here, I promise," said Mother Miriam Ruth, holding the girl firmly by one hand and positioning the large candle on the floor with the other. "I'll be right back. I'm going for chairs."

"No! Don't go! Please!" cried Sister Agnes, clutching at the older woman's habit.

"I said I'd be right back and I will. I'll be here with you the whole time. Now let me go, Agnes, please. We have to have chairs. There's nothing to this room to sit on."

"Don't bring more than two; I won't be needing one," Dr. Livingston called after her. Then she turned her attention to the young nun.

"Agnes, there's nothing to be afraid of. You'll go to sleep for a little while and I'll ask you some questions, and that's all."

But the girl's eyes remained wide, even after the mother superior had returned to the chamber. This was so different from anything she'd encountered before. Here she was, late at night while the rest of the convent was sleeping, sitting in the middle of a room she hadn't even known existed. Yet, for all her fear, when the doctor spoke to her in that soothing voice, Agnes closed her eyes and allowed Dr. Livingston's words to wash over her.

"You're relaxed . . . you're listening to a chorus

of angels. The music surrounds you like a warm
and comfortable pool of water. It covers your
mouth, your nose, your eyes. When I count to
three, you'll wake up. Can you hear me?"

"Yes." Agnes was under, in a hypnotic trance.

"Who am I?"

"Dr. Livingston."

"And why am I here?"

"To help me," said the girl dreamily.

"Good. Would you like to tell me why you're
here?"

"Because I'm in trouble."

"What kind of trouble?" asked Martha.

There was no answer, but the young nun's lips
began to tremble. Mother Miriam had placed Agnes's chair in the center of the room, under the
skylight, and a thin ray of filtered moonlight, paler
than the candle, made a small bright puddle on
the floor at her feet.

"What kind of trouble, Agnes?" asked the doctor again, more insistently.

The faraway dreamy quality of Agnes's voice
disappeared completely, and it became that of a
bewildered little girl. "I'm frightened."

"Of what?" Martha pressed.

"Of telling you."

Dr. Livingston lowered her voice, making it
even more gentle. "But it's easy. It's only a breath
of air with sound. Say it. What kind of trouble,
Agnes?"

Mother Miriam Ruth held her breath, her eyes
never leaving the girl's face.

"I had a baby," Agnes said.

A tiny sigh escaped the doctor. At last. Deep inside Agnes's subconscious, the fatal acknowledgment did indeed lie buried. Now perhaps they could bring it to the light, rid the girl of her fearful burden of guilt and pain, and find out what really happened that night the baby was born and died.

"How did you have a baby?"

"It came out of me," answered Agnes in a very low voice.

"Did you know it was going to come out?" asked the psychiatrist.

"Yes."

Martha and Mother Miriam Ruth exchanged a long, silent look. Then the doctor turned back to the young nun.

"Did you want it to come out?"

"No."

"Why?"

"Because I was afraid." And, reliving that night's terror now in her state of sleep, Agnes contorted her features in remembered fear.

"Why were you afraid?"

"Because I wasn't worthy."

"To be a mother?"

"Ye . . . yes." It was as if the answer had been dragged out of her. The girl's face began to crumple, and a tear formed in her eyes.

"Why?" asked Martha again, inexorable.

Agnes was crying now, shaking her head and

turning around as if seeking an escape. But Dr. Livingston was there, prodding her to remember.

"May I open my eyes now?" begged the girl.

"Not yet," said Martha gently. "Very soon but not yet. Do you know how the baby got into you?"

"It grew," sobbed Sister Agnes.

"What made it grow? Do you know?"

"Yes."

Another look passed between the psychiatrist and the mother superior. "Would you like to tell me?" asked Martha.

"No!" Agnes sobbed, wringing her hands in her lap. A small moan of sympathy escaped Mother Miriam Ruth, who stifled it at once, then grasped the crucifix on her breast and automatically whispered a "Hail, Mary."

But Dr. Livingston could not possibly let up now. She was aware that hypnotic recall was a painful process, leaving the subconscious raw and bleeding. But it was necessary surgery, if Agnes was to be helped. "Did anyone else know about the baby?" she demanded.

The hypnotized girl squirmed in her seat as though skewered there like an insect impaled by a pin. "I can't tell you that!" she moaned.

"Will she be angry?"

"She made me promise not to!" cried the nun.

"Who? Who made you promise?"

But a choked cry was Agnes's only answer. Tears glistened on her face, catching the moonlight and the light cast by the single candle. Her hands twisted together, writhing with a life of their own.

Abruptly, Martha abandoned this line of questioning. Sensing that it had led about as far as it was going to for the moment and that Sister Agnes was too agitated to answer questions like "who?" and "why?", she changed her tack.

"All right, Agnes," she said soothingly. "Let's go to your room. It's the night about six weeks ago, when you were very sick."

"I'm afraid!" The girl's voice quavered, and her closed eyelids fluttered nervously.

"Don't be," Martha said in a very low voice. "I'm here. All right?"

Agnes nodded. Even in her hypnotic trance, she sensed the doctor's soothing presence and was reassured by the sound of her voice.

"Tell me what you did before you went to bed."

"I ate," the girl replied in a much stronger voice. She had stopped squirming and was no longer sobbing. Her words came from somewhere very far away. The trance appeared to deepen.

"What did you have for dinner?"

"Fish. Brussels sprouts." The girl's nose wrinkled in disgust.

"You don't like brussels sprouts?"

"I hate them," answered Agnes, making a face.

"And then what happened?"

"We went to chapel for vespers. I left early because I wasn't feeling very well. . . ." She broke off and stiffened suddenly, sitting up very straight, ears straining.

"What is it?" asked the doctor.

"Someone's following me."

"Who?"

"Sister Marguerite, I think." She looked about her anxiously although her eyes were still closed.

"Was it Sister Marguerite who knew about the baby?"

But Agnes only turned away, refusing to answer. Her resistance to that question was still very strong, even under hypnosis.

Once more, Dr. Livingston changed her line of questioning. "Open your eyes, Agnes," she commanded. "I want you to see your room as you saw it on that night."

Slowly, the lids fluttered upward, and Agnes opened her eyes. She stared straight in front of her, still in a deep hypnotic state.

"What do you see?" Martha asked softly.

"My bed."

"What else?"

"A crucifix," breathed the nun, looking suddenly exalted.

"Above the bed?"

"Yes."

"Anything else?" asked the doctor.

Agnes leaned forward into the little puddle of moonlight as though searching for something.

"What do you see? Something different?"

The girl nodded.

"What is it?" Martha demanded, holding her breath.

"A wastepaper basket."

The psychiatrist let her breath out very slowly. She felt a prickle along her arms and at the back of her neck.

We're getting close, so close.

"Do you know who put it there?"

"No," Agnes said faintly. She sounded as though she was ill and in pain.

"Why do you think it's there?" persisted Martha.

"For me to get sick in." The girl grimaced. A sudden whimper of pain escaped her and she clutched at her belly with both hands.

"Are you ill?"

"Yes!" gasped Agnes. Sweat was beginning to roll down her forehead as she wrapped her arms tightly around herself and rocked back and forth, moaning with the onset of labor.

"What do you feel?"

A violent contraction suddenly shook the nun's thin body. She wrapped her arms tightly around herself and cried out in her pain. "I feel as if I've eaten glass!"

"What do you do?"

"I have to throw up." Shivering with the effort, Agnes managed to stand up from her chair. She staggered toward the imaginary wastebasket and threw herself onto her knees beside it, retching. But nothing came out.

"I can't," she moaned, then shrieked as another violent contraction seized her. "It's glass!" she screamed. "One of the sisters has fed me glass!"

"Oh, dear God," moaned Mother Miriam Ruth, and started to stand up, but a sharp gesture from Dr. Livingston forced her back into her chair again.

"Which sister fed you glass?" demanded Martha.

Agnes was weeping now, her body racked by convulsive sobs, as fresh waves of pain washed over her. "I don't *know* which one!" she wailed. "They're all jealous, that's why."

"Of what?"

"Of me!"

Another labor pang shook her, followed almost immediately by yet another one, even more violent and painful. "Oh, God!" she screamed. "Oh, my God!"

Mother Miriam Ruth stood up again, her arms automatically reaching out to the girl, but she didn't attempt to interfere. She shot an angry look at Dr. Livingston, but the psychiatrist didn't notice. All her attention was on Sister Agnes. Martha, too, was suffering for the girl, but there was nothing she could do about it. Agonizing as it was, this hypnosis was the beginning of healing and must be followed through to the bitter end.

Now Sister Agnes was patting at the skirts of her habit, confused and bewildered. "Water. It's all water." She was reliving the moment that her water had broken.

"Why doesn't anyone come?" asked Martha.

"They can't hear me!" gasped Agnes, doubling over with a fresh contraction. "Oh, no, please! I don't want this to happen! I don't *want* it!"

Dear Jesus, thought Mother Miriam Ruth, isn't it bad enough she had to go through this a first time? Does she have to relive it, with the same agony and the same terror? Can't she be spared at least some of this? She couldn't tear her eyes away from the girl, who was writhing and screaming as a new contraction, incredibly severe, gripped her and tore her apart. Please, God, help her, thought the mother superior. As though to echo her thoughts, Agnes cried out again and again, "Oh, God! Oh, my God!"

Doubled over, Sister Agnes was drenched in sweat and shivering. Her throat was raw with screaming, and she could only gasp for breath between the onslaught of each fresh wave of pain and the next.

Suddenly, the girl stiffened and sat up, as though seeing somebody. Her breath came in great gasps, with a ragged effort. Dr. Livingston leaned forward eagerly.

"What is it? What do you see?"

"Get away from me!" cried Agnes, her face distorted by fear.

"Who?" demanded the doctor.

But Sister Agnes stared ahead of her, focused on whatever or whoever it was that she was seeing. "Go away! I don't want you here!" she cried out.

"Is there someone in the room with you?"

"Don't touch me! Don't touch me!" shrieked the girl in terror, backing away as though the unseen threat was a mortal one. "Please! Please don't touch me!" she begged, weeping.

Mother Miriam Ruth could take no more. She rushed forward, catching up Agnes in her arms as another contraction hit her. "Stop her!" she shouted at the psychiatrist. "She'll hurt herself!"

"No!" Martha ordered sharply. "Let her go!"

"I'm not going on with this!" The mother superior's grasp tightened on the girl's arms.

"No!" yelled Martha, starting forward.

But Agnes was screaming and flailing her arms, pushing Mother Miriam Ruth away with surprising strength. "You're trying to take my baby! You're trying to take my baby!" she shrieked at the mother superior, tearing herself out of the older nun's grip.

Mother Miriam Ruth backed away, eyes wide. "No!"

The girl's hands were between her legs now, pushing hard at the baby's head, trying to force it back into her own body.

"Stay in! Please stay in!" But another labor pain, the most severe one yet, shook her body violently. She screamed in agony, rolling on the floor, and her scream was echoed by Mother Miriam Ruth's.

"Stop her!" begged the mother superior helplessly, turning her painracked face to Dr. Livingston. "Help her!"

"It's not my fault!" sobbed Agnes hysterically. "It's not my fault, Mummy! It's a mistake! Mummy, it's a mistake!"

There was too much pain in the room. Martha felt something snap inside her. She took a quick forward step, knelt on the floor beside Agnes, and clasped the girl in her arms.

"Agnes, it's all right. One, two, three. It's all right."

At the words *one, two, three,* Sister Agnes relaxed out of her trance. Swaying back and forth weakly, she would have fallen flat on the floor if the doctor hadn't been there to hold on to her.

"It's me, Dr. Livingston. It's all right."

But the girl still trembled; holding her tightly, Martha soothed her as she would a crying baby, with quiet, whispered words of reassurance and soft pats on her back and shoulders.

"Thank you. Thank you. How do you feel?"

"Frightened," Agnes whispered back.

Mother Miriam Ruth, anxious and jealous, longed to be the one comforting Agnes. That was not only her duty, it was her right. She remembered the girl's violent rejection of her in her hypnotic state, and seeing her now with Martha Livingston while she herself stood here ignored, the mother superior was both furious and envious.

"It's hard enough to go through it once, isn't it? Let alone twice?"

"Yes."

"You were very brave. Do you remember what just happened?"

"Yes," the girl answered, with a slight shudder.

"Good. Do you feel well enough to stand?"

Agnes nodded. Martha let go of her, and the nun stood up, slowly and carefully. The psychiatrist smiled at her proudly, as a parent does when an infant takes a step.

"There!"

Agnes leaned forward and threw her arms around the doctor gratefully. Between the two a strong link had been forged, out of agony and catharsis. And it was a strange link, too, for as Sister Agnes had been freed from some of her secret burden, the doctor had assumed that burden and had therefore become even more tightly bound.

Twelve

Who am I, Nancy Drew? thought Martha to herself, only half joking. I shouldn't be spending all this time trying to solve a mystery. I should be in my office with my own patients, or I won't have a private practice left to go back to! But now that I've managed to get Agnes to face the fact that there was a birth at all, the next step is to find out how the hell it happened. Since I've become familiar with the convent, I can well understand how the mother superior can claim that no outsider could penetrate its defenses. A mouse would have a better chance at a cat convention. But there has to be a way. Either Agnes got out or somebody got in or those three wise men rode in out of the east on camels after all.

Because the police had considered the case to

be cut and dried, because the indictment of Agnes had been so swift and so sure, nobody had bothered to investigate the "how" of the conception. Who the man was or how he managed to get close enough to Sister Agnes to father a child on her didn't matter to the outside world.

But it matters to me, thought Martha. Everything about this damn case matters to me. I'm in it up to my neck now, and I'll stick that neck out a mile if I have to.

She wasn't sure where she should start, but a government bureau seemed to be as good a place as any. There were files on anything and everything from Indian fishing rights to the zoning laws of downtown Montreal, all locked up in dusty cabinets in musty public buildings; almost nobody ever bothered to check them out.

Such a building housed the "Provincial Archives, Architecture, Lands Dept., Province of Quebec."

The archives were housed in one large room that smelled of stale paper and unwashed windows. There were tall shelves, reaching almost to the eleven-foot ceilings, and these were stacked high with rolled maps and surveyors' documents. Shelf after shelf of Canadian history was recorded and rolled and stored away here, never to be referred to again.

A man, the librarian, was sitting behind a desk not far from the door, immersed in a copy of *Cahiers du Cinema*. He glanced up, startled as

Dr. Livingston entered, as though he wasn't used to anybody coming in that door.

"Excuse me," began Martha, "I'm looking for some ground plans for St. Mary Magdalene's convent in Berthierville."

The librarian put down his film magazine and his face brightened. *"Ah, oui. C'est un héritage. Je crois qu'il date du dix-neuvième siècle. Suivez-moi, s'il vous plait."*

Standing up, he led the way over to the dusty stacks. Martha wondered how he could possibly know what was where. Yet he seemed to be familiar with all the stored-up history because within minutes he had pulled a large scroll off one shelf and was unrolling it on the map table.

"Le couvent des Petites Soeurs de Marie Magdalene," he announced, as the scroll unrolled far enough to be seen as a ground plan. *"Pourquoi avez-vous besoin de ceci?"* He shot her a sharp look over the rims of his glasses.

"J'écris une étude des couvents," lied Dr. Livingston. She couldn't tell him why she really needed it, though she knew her excuse was pretty lame.

Now the plan was fully unrolled, and the librarian pored over it, happy in his element. *"Très intéressant,"* he mused. *"Ce document contient tout, même les entrées secrètes."*

Secret entrances! The psychiatrist's ears perked up, and she followed, fascinated, the librarian's finger as he traced the route of the hidden passage.

"They all had them, all the convents," he told

her in French. "Usually to get from building to building in the snow. Like that one." He pointed to a dotted line on the map.

"That's how he got in," muttered Martha to herself in English. Immediately, the librarian cast her a suspicious glance.

"Pardonnez-moi, qu'est-ce que vous avez dit?"

"Rien, rien," answered Martha hastily. *"Merci mille fois,"* she added, picking up her purse and gloves. She was nearly running as she left the room, and she actually did run down the two long flights to the street, feeling—much to her own surprise—very like Nancy Drew after all.

As soon as she got to her car, Dr. Livingston copied everything she'd learned into the notebook she always carried with her. Now all she had to do was to trace the route shown on the ground plan's dotted line. But what if it no longer existed? After all, the convent was a century and a half old; it was quite likely that the "secret passage" hadn't been used for fifty years or more. Wouldn't Mother Miriam Ruth have mentioned it if she knew about it? Or was this one more example of how she was shielding Sister Agnes and trying to keep Dr. Livingston away from the truth?

Martha thought briefly of telling the mother superior what she intended to look for but dismissed it from her mind. Mother Miriam Ruth might forbid her. No, shoot first and ask questions afterward.

On the way to Berthierville, Martha went over in her mind the secret path traced by the dotted line that led from the convent to the outside world. When a scowling Sister Marguerite admitted her through the iron gate, she made directly for the chapel. The dotted line began there, in a room directly below the chapel altar.

But where? The walls appeared to be made of solid stone, no little wooden doors, no rings of iron that could be handles. The floor was also stone. The only illumination was from the few candles that burned before a small shrine in the corner in front of a statue of Saint Michael holding a sword.

Saint Michael. Martha thought for a moment. Wasn't he the angel who guarded the Garden of Eden? Yes, it was he who drove Adam and Eve out with his flaming sword at the command of God. Guarding the portals, the sword in his right hand, his left hand by his side, but ... Martha felt her heart beating faster ... his left forefinger was *pointing downward.*

She approached the statue, her eyes following the pointing finger. A low stone archway stood off to the left, not visible from the rest of the room. Past the archway, a narrow dark set of stone steps led below. It was well concealed and very dark.

Martha took a candle from the stand in front of the holy statue. Ducking her head so that she wouldn't bump it on the low arch stone, she made her way down the steps.

The steps led to an abandoned crypt, where the first nuns of the Little Sisters of Mary Magdalene had been buried in the early days of the convent. The crypt had long been abandoned in favor of the newer cemetery, and dust, cobwebs, and small nameless animals had claimed it for their own. The tombstones had cracked; the dust on them had by now lain thick and undisturbed for more than a century. A narrow dirt path led between the rows of stone sarcophagi, and Martha followed it. She'd never seen tombs like these up close, but they were similar to ancient Etruscan tombs she'd visited on trips to Italy.

Curious, Martha paused by one of the tombs and brushed the dirt off, holding the candle close to see the inscription. It read: SOEUR JESUS MATILDE, 1772–1856, DEUS SALVAT. A good long life, she thought, and probably a lot less complicated than she'd have today.

But she had to keep going; besides, the stale and musty smell of the crypt was beginning to overcome her. At the far end of the crypt, she could see the opening of the tunnel—the secret passage that led to the outside. This was what she'd come for, to find the way out, the way that Sister Agnes must have taken that night of January 23, the night that Sister Paul died and Agnes conceived a child.

The tunnel was long and dark. The darkness didn't faze Martha; she was too rational to be afraid of the dark. But there were little rustling noises coming from ahead, and the scrabble of tiny claws. At best mice, at worst rats. Rats were pretty scary, even to the rational mind. Martha took a deep breath.

Whatever's in there, it's probably more afraid of me than I am of it, she reminded herself.

She plunged into the mouth of the tunnel, just managing to keep her candle from extinguishing. There was an overwhelming odor of stale animal droppings and other smells that Martha preferred not to think about, but she managed to breathe mostly through her mouth. How long the tunnel was, or how many minutes she was in it, she had only the vaguest idea. Perhaps five, perhaps ten minutes. Distances and time spent in the dark are deceiving.

. She tried, as she walked hesitantly along, to imagine Sister Agnes following this path. She tried to put herself into Agnes's situation, to get inside her head. Was she frightened, alone down here in the blackness? Did she have fantasies of a descent into hell? Or was heaven waiting at the other end? Did Agnes know what she was moving toward, step by step?

Other questions occurred to Dr. Livingston. If this tunnel *was* the one used by Agnes that night, how did she find out about it? Did the man, whoever he was, tell her? Had they met before? Or was the existence of the tunnel common knowledge in the convent, a knowledge kept only from herself, because she was an outsider?

The tunnel was coming to an end now. It was widening into a small square space. A dead end. This was ridiculous; tunnels don't lead to absolutely nowhere. Unless this one had been blocked off decades ago. In which case, there goes my whole damn theory down the drain, Martha thought.

Martha held the candle up high and cast its thin flicker around the small room. There! Yes, up there in the low ceiling, just over her head. A wooden trapdoor, held by three bolts. Standing on tiptoe, the doctor threw the bolts one at a time. They moved with little resistance; evidently they had been in recent use. Flinging the trapdoor open with an effort, she pulled herself up through it and rested, panting, on her elbows.

After the pitch blackness of the tunnel, the strong light of an early November afternoon dazzled the psychiatrist, making her squint. For a minute she had no idea where she was; all she had was the impression of a vast open space and strong light. And it was cold, bitter cold. Then, suddenly, she knew.

It was the barn. The large, empty, unused barn. That's where the tunnel came up. Of course. In the old days, it linked the convent to its animals. In the icy winters, the nuns could feed them and milk them without venturing out into the high drifts of snow. Nowadays, with only one cow and that cow kept in the little stable, it could be the perfect situation for a rendezvous.

Was it to this place that Sister Agnes came on the night of January 23, as Sister Paul, her only friend, lay dying?

Martha Livingston left the convent without seeing either Agnes or Mother Miriam Ruth. She needed some time to digest the significance of her discovery and to think of how best to approach Agnes with her knowledge.

But she wasn't to be given that time.

Mother Miriam Ruth had been so upset by the hypnotism session that she'd contacted the bishop at once. And when on the following day she'd learned from Sister Anne that the psychiatrist had come to the convent but had not asked for her or conferred with her before leaving, the mother superior's indignation knew no limits. She telephoned the bishop again, requesting, even demanding, an immediate appointment.

Which was granted. His Excellency sent his own personal limousine to Berthierville to bring Mother Miriam Ruth, accompanied by Sister Anne, to his cathedral in Montreal. Their meeting was brief and to the point, and ended with the two of them in perfect agreement. It only remained to inform Dr. Livingston of their decision.

It would give the mother superior great pleasure to be the one to do so, and His Excellency was gracious in granting it. Back into the limousine the two nuns climbed and were driven to the downtown office of Dr. Martha Livingston.

Helen Gervaise, Martha's secretary and receptionist, was typing up the doctor's tapes when a grim-faced nun, followed by a smaller, more timid one, barged into the office without ceremony. Immersed in her tapes and with the headphones on, Helen didn't look up until the nun rapped sharply on her desk.

"Is the doctor in her office?" demanded Mother Miriam Ruth.

"Who shall I say is calling?"

"General MacArthur," snapped the nun, and marched past her and a waiting patient toward the door to Martha's private office.

"Hey! Just a minute!" protested Helen. "You can't go in there! Please!"

But it was too late to stop her. Leaving Sister Anne behind in the waiting room, Mother Miriam Ruth had already opened Martha's door. By the time the receptionist caught up with her, she was halfway into the inner office.

"That's all right, Helen," called Martha in answer to her secretary's guilty shrug. "Just close the door, please." She looked questioningly at the mother superior, who got directly to the point without an opening greeting.

"I just met with the bishop, and we're taking you off the case."

"Taking me off the case? What are you talking about? You can't take me off the case. I'm court-appointed."

"If we want to hire a psychiatrist for Agnes, we'll find our own, thank you."

"Who'll ask the questions that *you* want asked," Martha shot at her.

Bridling, Mother Miriam Ruth retorted, "One who will approach this matter with some objectivity and respect!"

"For the Church?" demanded the furious Dr. Livingston.

"For Agnes!"

Martha's eyes narrowed. "You think she's a saint?"

Mother Miriam Ruth's back stiffened and her chin came up. "She's been touched by God, yes."

This admission forced an explosion from Martha. "How?" she yelled. "She hallucinates, stops eating, and bleeds spontaneously. Is that supposed to convince me that she shouldn't be *touched*? Give me a miracle!"

For a moment the nun stood speechless, considering whether to say to this psychiatrist what she had in her mind. Then, taking a deep breath, she dived in headfirst. "The father . . ."

"Who is he?" interrupted Martha eagerly.

"Why must he be anybody?"

Wordless, the doctor stared at the mother superior, until the nun's words, in all their significance, sank in. Then she burst into laughter. "Oh, my God"—she laughed—"you're as crazy as the rest of your family."

Not having expected this reaction, Mother Miriam Ruth looked hurt and confused. "I don't know if it's true, I . . . I only think that . . . it might be possible. . . ."

"How?" Martha snorted scornfully. "Do you think a big white dove came flying through her window?"

"Don't be ridiculous!" cried the mother superior, offended.

"Then give me a reasonable explanation," demanded the doctor.

"A miracle is an event *without* an explanation. If she's capable of putting a hole in her hand without benefit of a nail, why couldn't she split a cell in her womb?"

Martha closed her eyes in exasperation, every rational fiber of her being protesting this antiscientific outrage. "This is insane!"

But Mother Miriam Ruth was rolling, and there was no stopping her now as she warmed to her theory. "There was no man at the convent on that night, and there was no way for any man to get in or out." She shut her lips tightly, as though her case was proven and closed.

"So you're saying God did it," observed Martha with one eyebrow up.

"No!" the mother superior declared passionately. "That's as much as saying Father Martineau did it. I'm saying God permitted it."

"But how did it happen?" insisted Dr. Livingston.

Mother Miriam Ruth looked beatific. "You'll never find the answer to everything, Doctor. For every miracle science explains, ten thousand more come into being."

"I thought you didn't believe in miracles today."

"I want the opportunity to believe. I want the choice to believe," the nun breathed earnestly.

Martha stood up and faced the mother superior eye to eye. Speaking slowly and with great emphasis, she said, "What you are choosing to believe is a lie. Because you don't want to face the fact that Agnes was raped, or seduced, or that she did the seducing."

The nun recoiled as if struck. "She's an innocent!" she protested.

"But she's not an enigma. Everything that Agnes has done is explainable by modern psychiatry. One, two, three, right down the line."

"Is that what you believe?" demanded Mother Miriam Ruth. "That she's the sum total of her psychological parts?"

"That's what I have to believe," the doctor said quietly.

"Then why are you so obsessed with her?" hissed the nun, and an expression of satisfaction crossed her face when she saw Dr. Livingston flinch. "You're losing sleep," she charged, "thinking of her all the time, bent on saving her. Why? That's a question, no answer needed."

Mother Miriam Ruth turned to leave in triumph. It was time for Martha Livingston to play her hole card.

"There's a tunnel out of the crypt into the

barn. Did you know about that?" she asked
softly.

The mother superior turned, and surprise was
evident on her features.

"There *is* an answer," Martha threw at the
nun. "That's how she got out."

Mother Miriam Ruth made a dismissive gesture with her right hand. "That's crazy," she
said flatly. "How could she find out something
like that?"

"Somebody told her."

"Who? That tunnel hasn't been used in fifty
years?"

Pushed to her limits, Martha exploded. "Stop
lying, Mother!" she yelled.

"Why would I lie?" asked the mother superior
blandly.

"Because this is murder we're talking about!"

Like a hostile missile, the word fell between
them. Mother Miriam Ruth gasped. "Murder?"

"Aren't you concerned about what she told
us?" the psychiatrist cried hotly. "About that
other person in the room?"

"I'm concerned about her health and safety!"
the nun flung angrily back at the doctor.

"Who was that other person, Mother?" hissed
Martha. "Was it you?"

But Mother Miriam Ruth withdrew from the
argument. "If you believe this is murder," she
said slowly and with dignity, "then it's the Crown
attorney you have to talk to. Not me. And definitely not Agnes." She marched to the door.

"Wait!" called Martha after her. "Where are you going?"

But all the psychiatrist saw was a retreating back in a black habit, and all she heard was the slam of a door.

Thirteen

Martha was desperate. She didn't underestimate for one minute the bishop's power to have her taken off the case, court-appointed or not. He was an influential man in Quebec, but especially so in Montreal. If Mother Miriam Ruth had already delivered the triumphant announcement, the chances were good that the bishop had not only set the wheels in motion, but that they were rolling over her this very minute.

She was right. As soon as the mother superior had marched out of her office in a storm of righteous indignation, Martha got on the phone to the courthouse. The evasiveness in the voice of Justice Leveau's secretary was enough to put her on her guard immediately, and when Miss Hilliard added, "We've sent you a letter, Dr. Livingston.

You should be receiving it tomorrow," Martha realized she'd have to act fast. Grabbing her jacket and purse, she almost ran out of her office, apologizing over her shoulder to the waiting patient she was standing up, and drove at once to the courthouse.

Justice Leveau was just leaving his office when she dashed in, out of breath. One look at his black robes and Martha knew he was on his way to court. Her heart sank.

"I have no time for you now, Martha." He waved her off. "I've sent you a letter, but if you can't wait for it, ask Miss Hilliard to show you a copy."

"Joe, please, don't do this."

But he was off and striding down the marble hall to his courtroom. In a hurry, distracted by thoughts of the case he was about to hear, Leveau scowled at Dr. Livingston as she raced along with him, sticking firmly to his side.

"All I want is one more week!" she pleaded.

"Why?" Justice Leveau didn't break stride. "Mother Miriam Ruth is very adamant about this. You've done nothing to show any progress—"

"I'm a nuisance to her," interrupted the doctor.

"You're a nuisance to all of us, Martha. Let's face it," he growled.

"I'll have a decision in a week," Martha promised.

The judge lengthened his stride, as though to outrun the doctor. There was an expression of irritation on his normally placid features. "I would remind you, Dr. Livingston, that you never wanted to take on this case in the first place. It seems that you were right to demur. Now it's gone on long enough! You're out!"

"Joe!" They were just outside the courtroom door, and Martha was about to lose him and her chance for keeping the case. She was at the end of her rope. "She didn't kill the baby!" Her words echoed weirdly in the marble corridor, even more weirdly inside her brain.

Justice Leveau stopped at once and turned to face her, his eyes grave.

"You have proof?" he asked her sternly.

"I'll have it," vowed Martha.

"When?" he demanded.

"Next week."

Giving vent to a little sound of annoyance, Leveau turned away to enter his courtroom. "No, Martha—" he began wearily.

"Tomorrow!" Dr. Livingston cried. "I'll have it tomorrow!"

For an instant the judge hesitated, his foot over the threshold. Then he turned back to look at the psychiatrist. Martha's cheeks were flushed with anxiety, and her eyes were too bright. Leveau sighed; he wasn't an unkind man.

"Oui, bon. À demain," he said.

Now she had until tomorrow. But only until then.

For the first time in all her visits there, Martha found the convent gate unlocked and stand-

ing open. Also, there were other cars parked
outside, two battered old Fords and a shiny new
Chevrolet pickup truck stood alongside Father
Martineau's ancient Volvo. Something was going
on inside. For a minute, the doctor stood at the
gate, wondering whether to ring for Sister Marguerite, wondering whether Sister Marguerite
would let her come in. Then, taking the open
gate as an invitation to enter, she walked up the
gravel and in through the large wooden door,
similarly unlocked.

Nobody came to greet her or turn her away.
There was nobody in sight, nobody scrubbing
down the convent floors or carrying armloads of
clean laundry or simply gliding down the corri-
dors the way nuns do. But, from a distance, she
could hear the sound of voices raised in sacred
song. They were in the chapel.

Martha knew that she had no business to intrude on them, yet the voices were so beautiful
that they drew her to the chapel despite herself.
Above them all, she could hear the clear, pure
voice of Agnes, the voice that Mother Miriam
Ruth believed was her guardian angel restored to
her after so many years. The idea didn't seem
quite so farfetched now.

At the chapel door she paused, peering inside.
One look and she understood.

Today was the day that Sister Genevieve was
taking her final vows. The chapel was filled with
flowers, and flowers surrounded the novice, who
lay facedown on the floor, with her arms stretched

out, a living cross. She was dressed in bridal white for the celebration of her marriage to Christ.

Also garbed in white, Father Martineau stood above the prostrate girl, swinging a censer from which came perfumed smoke. It was heavy, and hard for him to lift, but he was assisted by a younger parish priest.

Mother Miriam Ruth knelt alone in a pew, her rosary wrapped around her fingers, head bent yet still with her eyes on Sister Genevieve. Was she thinking of the years in which the chapel floor was filled with prostrate novices giving themselves to Christ? Now there was only one, and next year there might be none at all.

In the front pews, smiling proudly, sat a small group of villagers dressed in their best, Genevieve's family, obviously farmers, obviously the owners of the old Fords and the new pickup. One woman was weeping openly, sobbing into a lace-trimmed handkerchief. This must be the girl's mother, surrendering her daughter for life to the authority of another mother, a mother superior.

The nuns were singing magnificently led by Agnes, whose exalted face outshone the candles before the altar and the saints.

> *Agnus Dei,*
> *qui tollis peccata mundi,*
> *miserere nobis.*
> *Agnus Dei,*
> *qui tollis peccata mundi,*
> *miserere nobis.*
> *Agnus Dei,*

qui tollit peccata mundi,
dona nobis pacem.

Lamb of God, who taketh away the sins of the
world, give us peace. . . .

I don't belong here, I'm trespassing in the worst possible way, Martha thought with a pang, and hurried away before anybody could discover her. Hurrying to her car, she drove off, going three or four miles into the countryside before she parked on a broad shoulder of the road and turned off the ignition.

She sat, her heart pounding, and tried to get her thoughts in order, attempting to identify and analyze her confused feelings. This would have been the perfect time for a cigarette, but Martha didn't have a pack with her. She hadn't smoked one since the night that she and Mother Miriam Ruth had sat smoking in the gazebo, playing that ridiculous game. Every now and then she missed them, even regretted giving them up, but most of the time she was satisfied to be without nicotine and grateful that she could do without it as a crutch.

What was that she had said to Agnes? "Smoking is an obsession with me. I guess I'll stop smoking when I become obsessed with something else."

I knew myself better than I thought I did, she now thought. I suppose I've transferred my obsession from the tobacco to the case. Or maybe directly to Agnes. Am I as obsessed with her as

Mother Miriam Ruth says I am? She accused me of losing sleep, of thinking of Agnes all the time. And she's right. I am bent on saving her.

The irony of the situation—of both women convinced of Agnes's innocence, for very different reasons—struck Martha as funny. Mother Miriam Ruth's obsession was Agnes's spiritual innocence while Martha was obsessed with proving her innocence before the law. The psychiatrist wanted to play detective and prove that Agnes didn't kill the baby. The nun wanted to play God and prove that Agnes was a verifiable saint. Which of them was right? Or were they both dead wrong?

Remembering her dream, Martha shuddered. Last night she had dreamed she was a midwife in a small private hospital in a faraway land. She was dressed in white and the room she was in was white, and a window was open and she could see mountains of snow all around her. Below her on a table lay a woman prepared for a cesarean. She began to scream, and Martha knew that she had to cut the baby out as quickly as possible. With a knife she cut a slit in the woman's belly, then reached inside, up to her wrists. Suddenly, she felt a tiny hand grab hold of her fingers and begin to pull.

And as the woman's hands pressed down on my head, the little creature inside drew me in, to the elbows, to the shoulders, to the chin . . . But when I opened my mouth to scream—

She woke up, and found that her sheets were

spotted with her blood. Menstrual blood. Her cycle, which had always been sporadic but which had ceased three years before, had returned.

She had felt as though something important, something that had been taken from her, had been restored. And despite the ugliness and terror of the dream, Martha Livingston felt marvelous, better than she'd felt in ages.

Martha let herself dwell for a minute or two on the ceremony she'd just witnessed. It hadn't been the first she'd seen. Years ago, it had been her sister Marie lying there facedown, on the floor of Montreal Cathedral, surrounded by thirty other novices taking their vows. A large chorus of nuns had sung the Gloria then, too, and instead of two plain country priests, the archbishop himself had celebrated the mass.

It all came flooding back. Her mother's pride, and her own anger. She was losing her one and only sister to an unenlightened and medieval institution; Marie was leaving the real world, where she could have made a place for herself, to join an order that would keep her apart from reality. Martha had been deeply angry, but her rage then was nothing compared to her fury when she learned of her sister's death less than a year later.

For more than twenty years, she had carried this anger around inside her, and it had cast its dark shadow upon her life. And certainly on her approach to Agnes and the mother superior and this case.

Now, for the first time in all those years, she felt the burden of that anger lifted from her soul. Seeing that poor little novice taking her vows today had somehow set Martha free of her memories. Perhaps it was the exaltation of the ancient ceremony, and the pride on the faces of those humble relatives into whose life a little importance and beauty had been shed this morning. Perhaps it was Father Martineau's words coming back to her. In his halting Greek, he had said, "Judge not, lest ye be judged."

All these years, I have judged not only that stupid mother superior, but also my sister. I have held her to blame for her own death, but who am I to make that judgment? We all pursue what we think will make us happy. How could I dare to consider Marie's pursuit less valid, less meaningful than my own? She could no more live a life like mine than I could live a life like hers. Now who's to say she was wrong? I can't, not anymore.

She felt tears of relief springing to her eyes, relief and something very like joy. And something more: a decisiveness stronger than before.

She was still determined to prove Sister Agnes innocent. She was still determined to make Mother Miriam Ruth tell the truth Martha knew she was concealing. But all the old festering anger was gone, burned out. It was no longer relevant; it never really was. At last Martha could confront Agnes and Mother Miriam Ruth without seeing the ghosts of other nuns over their shoulders.

She went through all the facts again, dwelling intently on the wastepaper basket. Suddenly it struck her. At last she remembered what there was about the wastepaper basket that had eluded her before. Not only was Agnes the only nun to have one, but the wastepaper basket in Mother Miriam Ruth's office, the one she'd flicked her cigarette ashes into days before, was so small. Too small; Martha had noted the fact subconsciously without registering it in her conscious mind. Only a little wire basket, standing where a large solid basket ought to be standing. In fact, *had* been standing. Another piece of the puzzle fitted into place. It must have been Mother Miriam Ruth's wastebasket that was in Agnes's room the night the baby was born. And it was there because the mother superior had put it there. This was an important part of the proof that she had promised Leveau, evidence of Agnes's innocence. If Sister Agnes was innocent of killing her baby, it meant only one thing. That somebody else was guilty.

The ceremony must be over by now, the mass celebrated, the novice a nun with a wedding band on her finger. It was time to go back.

The gate was locked again. Sister Marguerite unlocked it, scowling furiously, but refused to allow Dr. Livingston to enter the convent door.

"Wait here," she muttered angrily, and went to tell the mother superior.

The front door was ajar, and from inside Martha could hear the sounds of a wedding party, laughter and French Canadian folk songs being played on an accordion. Remembering her own sister's celebration, she knew that there would be a wedding cake with white icing, and that Sister Genevieve would be dancing in her white wedding gown, with flowers in her hair. *On their wedding day, all brides are beautiful, even Sister Genevieve.*

Mother Miriam Ruth appeared in the doorway, her face as cold and hard as quarried marble.

"I thought I told you—" she began, but Martha reached silently into her purse and handed the mother superior a letter, its envelope embossed with the official seal of the Canadian judiciary.

The nun took it without a word, ripped the envelope open, and scanned its contents. It was Justice Leveau's official authorization for Dr. Martha Livingston to resume her psychiatric duties in the case of Sister Agnes of the Convent of the Little Sisters of Saint Mary Magdalene in Berthierville, Province of Quebec. There was no word in it about Martha's having only one day, and Martha didn't see fit to mention it to Mother Miriam Ruth.

"This is permission to take her apart," Mother Miriam Ruth commented bitterly.

"Where is she?" asked Martha.

"Hasn't she had enough?" cried the nun, her large dark eyes pleading.

"I want to ask her a few questions," the doctor replied.

"My God, but you're determined!"

"Who knew that she was pregnant?" asked Martha calmly.

"If you're going to continue to persecute us—"

"Was it you?" interrupted the psychiatrist.

"She's a nun, and you hate nuns . . ."

"Did you know that she was pregnant?" insisted Martha.

"Yes!"

The single word hung in the air, echoing. Behind them, inside the convent, music. Outside, the autumn silence broken by the sound of birds cawing and the word *yes*.

Furious with Martha, furious with herself, Mother Miriam Ruth ran out into the yard, as though she could escape this doctor and her hounding questions. But there was no hope of that. Dr. Livingston followed her, still pelting her with questions which the mother superior knew she had to answer.

"You didn't send her to a doctor?"

"I didn't guess until it was too late."

"For what?" demanded Martha. "An abortion?"

"Don't be absurd," snapped the nun.

"Too late for what?" Unrelenting, the psychiatrist bore down on her like a drill bit.

Mother Miriam Ruth's face crumpled, and tears stung her eyelids. "I don't know!" she cried. "Too late to stop it!"

"The baby?"

"The scandal! I had to have time to think."

"You went to her room to help with the birth," Martha prompted.

The nun shook her head. "Agnes didn't want help," she said faintly.

"But you wanted the child out of the way," insisted the doctor.

"That's a lie!" The mother superior's voice cracked a little from the strain she was under.

"You hid the wastepaper basket in the room," continued Martha, coming closer to Mother Miriam Ruth. Her nerves were raw and tingling; she felt so close to the truth that she could almost reach out and take it into her hand.

"I didn't hide it!" denied the nun. "I put it there for the blood and the dirty sheets—"

"And the baby!" cried Martha.

"No!"

The psychiatrist's eyes were twin lasers. "You tied the cord around its neck—"

The veins in Mother Miriam Ruth's neck stood out, and her hands clenched the rosary at her waist. In a strangled voice, she answered, "I wanted her to have it when no one was around! I would have taken the baby to a hospital and left it with them. But there was so much blood, I panicked—"

"Before or after you killed the child?"

Mother Miriam Ruth's head was shaking vehemently from side to side. "I left the baby with Agnes! I went to get help!"

What is she saying? Martha thought. That Agnes killed the baby after all? If it wasn't Reverend Mother who tied that cord, who else could it be? They can't both be innocent.

"I doubt that's what Agnes would say." Martha's words issued from between grim lips.

Mother Miriam Ruth put both hands over her face, and her thin body convulsed, a long, shuddering movement.

"Then she's a goddamned liar!" she cried out, and burst into tears.

Fourteen

"Hello, Agnes."

"Hello."

"I have some more questions I'd like to ask you. Is that all right?"

"Yes."

"And I would like to hypnotize you again. Is that all right, too?"

"Yes."

Mother Miriam Ruth was present once again in the room under the convent roof, apart from all the others, when Martha hypnotized Agnes. The faintest sound of merriment came from downstairs as the wedding party drew to a close, and filtered light from the skylight above brightened the room, falling in straight shafts onto the chair in the center of the floor.

"Good," said Martha soothingly. "Sit down. Relax. You're going to enter that pool of water again. Only this time, I want you to imagine that there are holes in your body, and the warm water is flowing into those holes ... behind your eyes, warm, so warm, so clean, like prayer ... your eyes are so heavy ... so sleepy. Close your eyes. When I count to three, you'll wake up. Agnes, can you hear me?"

"Yes."

"Who am I?"

"Dr. Livingston."

"And who is with me?"

"Mother Miriam Ruth."

"Good. Agnes, I want you to remember, if you can, one night last January, the night Sister Paul died. Do you remember ... ?"

"Sister Paul. She said ... she said ..." The girl broke off, and tears sprang to her eyes.

"What's the matter?" Martha leaned forward eagerly. "What did Sister Paul tell you?"

"She said, 'Michael.' "

"What did she mean?"

"The statue."

"What statue?" asked Mother Miriam Ruth, mystified, but Dr. Livingston hushed her with a negative shake of the head.

"She'd shown it to me the day before," said Agnes from her hypnotic trance.

"And the passage to the barn?"

"Yes," answered Agnes.

From the mother superior came a sharp intake of breath; she was stunned that Agnes knew about it.

"Why did Sister Paul show you the passage?" asked the doctor softly.

"So I could go to Him!"

"Who?"

"Him!" From the exaltation on her face, Agnes's meaning could be clearly read.

"How did she know about Him?" Martha continued.

"She'd seen Him, too."

"Where?"

"From the bell tower. The day before she died." Martha recalled now that Agnes had told her, as the two of them had climbed the steep steps to the tower, that Sister Paul had died the day after she'd climbed up there for the last time. Martha imagined the scene that afternoon. . . .

They stood there together on the platform, the oldest and the youngest nun, friends. The day was very cold, even for January, but it was clearer than it had been in weeks. You could see for miles from the old bell tower, clear over the fields and almost into the village.

The old nun was dying, and she knew it. She wasn't afraid to die; in fact, she was ready. Jesus was waiting for her, waiting to take her into His arms. He was out there, beckoning to her, calling to her.

Come to Me, Sister Paul. Come to Me.

But she was so old, and so tired, and it was hard to breathe. She could see Christ the Dear

Lord from where she was standing, but she couldn't go to Him. It was so far, and her legs were so feeble. She'd never be able to reach Him.

Did that mean that she was lost? Would her soul never fly up to heaven? Sister Agnes here was so young, so strong. Her legs never seemed to tire. I'll send Sister Agnes to Him, Sister Paul thought. He is calling; I can see Him from here. Sister Agnes will go in my place, to tell Him I love Him and would be with Him myself if I could.

Martha could see that Agnes was remembering the day as well.

"And so she sent you?" Martha prompted gently.

"Yes."

"What happened?"

"I took a candle from the statue of Saint Michael. I know he will forgive me. It was very dark in the crypt, but the tunnel was even darker and more frightening. Something ran over my foot, and I cried out. . . ." Agnes's voice came from very far away.

"Yes . . . and?"

The trance appeared to deepen; the girl's eyelids fluttered rapidly as she relived the events of that night.

"I undo the bolts. They are very stiff, and I have to push very hard on them. There! The trapdoor is open now . . . I'm in the barn. It's so cold! But I don't think about the cold. He's here!"

"Are you frightened?" asked Martha.

"Yes. It's very dark in the barn, and I have only one little candle. I can hear the pigeons moving in the rafters; they're afraid, too. But there's another sound . . . Is it You?"

Mother Miriam Ruth grasped her crucifix and began to pray silently, her eyes never leaving Agnes's exalted face.

"He doesn't answer me. I know that I shouldn't be afraid, but I am. Very afraid. Then I hear Him. . . ."

She was deep inside the trance now, living again the events of that eerie night. When next she spoke, it was not to the psychiatrist, not to the mother superior, but to someone . . . or something . . . that only she could see and hear.

"Yes. Yes, I do." Again she listened for the voice.

"Why me?" she asked, a small whimper catching in her throat. "Wait! I want to see you!!" Her eyes were staring, straining from their sockets, and her bony hands stretched out in supplication.

"What do you see?" Dr. Livingston asked, fascinated. Mother Miriam Ruth stood frozen, her face drained of color, her lips reciting a paternoster by rote.

Sister Agnes smiled. "A flower, waxy and white," she said dreamily. "A drop of blood, sinking into the petal, flowing through the veins . . . halos, dividing and dividing . . . feathers are stars, falling . . . falling into the iris of God's eye."

Ecstasy had taken possession of Agnes, and she had no idea of where she was, either in the past or in the present. Martha had never seen her so ... translucent ... light seemed to shine through her and radiate from her.

"Oh, my God, He sees me!" she cried. "Oh, it's so lovely ... so blue, yellow, black wings, brown blood ... No, it's red, *His* blood. My God! My God!"

And she was shrieking now, in purest horror. Scream after scream. "I'm bleeding! I'm bleeding!" She sprang up from her chair, but she couldn't stand. She swayed briefly, then collapsed back into the chair again, moaning pitifully. At the same instant that Dr. Livingston and Mother Miriam Ruth moved to help her, they saw it.

Sister Agnes was bleeding from both palms.

Blood was flowing from her hands, down to the floor beside her chair. The girl herself was close to unconscious.

"Oh, my God!" breathed Martha, horror-stricken.

"Oh, dear Jesus Christ!" whispered Mother Miriam Ruth.

They stood frozen, watching the moaning girl in the chair, neither knowing what to do. But before they could take action of any kind, Agnes began to writhe, agitated.

"I have to wash this off," she babbled. "It's on my hands, my legs. My God, it won't stop! How do I make it stop?" But it wasn't the blood on her palms that so terrified her; it was her virgin blood, which had soaked through the sheets that night. The night that Sister Paul died, and Sister Agnes had surrendered herself to . . . whom? . . . what? . . . and had burned her sheets in fear.

Mother Miriam Ruth regained her composure and, capable of action again, took hold of Agnes, but the girl struggled fiercely, with an incredible strength she'd never before shown.

"Agnes, please . . ."

"Let go of me!"

"Agnes, you must let me help you!"

"Get away from me! I wish you were dead!" She pulled hard at the mother superior's fingers to loosen their hold on her arms. Her lips were drawn back in an animal snarl, exposing her small white teeth, which gleamed ferally.

Martha Livingston could see that Agnes was still in her hypnotic state, violently agitated though she was. She took a step toward her. "Agnes . . ."

"I wish you were all dead!" the girl shrieked, breaking loose from the two of them and running to a corner of the room, where she cowered like a trapped animal, panting in fear.

"Agnes, we had nothing to do with that man in the barn. . . . said Martha, following her.

"Let me alone!" roared Agnes. Her eyes were rolling in her head, and sweat was pouring over her forehead from under her wimple.

But Martha had no intention of letting her alone. She had to get through to her, to make her understand the truth about that night, to accept the truth, so that she could begin to deal with it. Only in that direction lay Agnes's salvation.

"He did a very bad thing to you. Do you understand?" She put one hand on Agnes's arm, but the girl shook it off.

"Don't touch me!"

"He frightened you, and he hurt you." The psychiatrist reached out again, but the nun shrank back.

"Don't!" she shrieked, unwilling even under hypnosis to hear what she was afraid to hear.

"It's not your fault. . . ."

"Mummy!" moaned Agnes.

"It's his fault," Martha told her.

"It's Mummy's fault!" the girl yelled, and turned angrily on Mother Miriam Ruth. "It's *your* fault!"

The mother superior took a horrified step back and seemed to shrink inside her habit. "No!" she wailed.

"Tell us who he is," urged the doctor, "so we can find him and stop him from doing this to other women. . . ."

But Agnes wasn't listening. She was glaring at Mother Miriam Ruth, and her small hands were clenched tightly into fists. "It's all your fault!" she cried again.

Martha stepped up to the girl and took her firmly by the shoulders to get her complete attention. "Agnes, who did you see in the room?" she demanded.

"I hate him!"

"Of course you do. Who was he?"

"I hate him for what he did to me!"

This was real. This was good. This was heal-ing. "Yes," said Dr. Livingston.

"For what he made me go through!" Agnes's breath was coming quickly, in short ragged bursts, fueled by her rage.

"Who?" pleaded Martha.

"I hate him!" The girl's face was a gorgon mask of loathing.

"Who did this to you?" Dr. Livingston insisted.

The young nun threw her head back as though she were going to howl like a starving wolf. Then she spit the words directly into the psychiatrist's face.

"God!" she shrieked. "It was God! And now I'll burn in hell because I hate Him!" The fren-zied pressure of her emotion hurled her into a storm of piteous weeping.

Martha's heart ached for Agnes's misery. "You won't burn in hell," she said softly but earnestly. "It's all right to hate Him."

"That's enough for today," put in Mother Mir-iam Ruth. "Wake her up." The mother superior looked exhausted, completely wrung out. Her face was very pale and there were smudges of black under her eyes.

"She doesn't belong to you anymore," Martha said quietly.

"She belongs to God."

"Agnes, what happened to the baby?" asked Martha, her eyes intent on the young nun's face.

"She can't remember!" said Mother Miriam Ruth, too quickly.

But from her trance, Sister Agnes said simply, "Yes," and waited for the psychiatrist's voice.

"She took the baby in her arms," said Martha, meaning Mother Miriam Ruth.

"Yes." Again, the voice from very far away.

"You saw it all, didn't you?"

"Yes."

"And then . . .what did she do?"

Agnes turned her face to look at the mother superior. Mother Miriam Ruth opened her lips to speak but shut them again without saying a word. Her dark eyes closed in suffering.

"Agnes, what did she do?" asked Dr. Livingston again.

"She left me alone with that little . . . thing," said Agnes very simply and quietly. "I looked at it and thought, this is a mistake. But it's *my* mistake, not Mummy's. I thought, I can save her. I can give her back to God."

Martha's throat suddenly went very dry. "What did you do?" she rasped.

"I put her to sleep," the girl said, smiling.

"How?" said Martha, dreading to hear the answer. A cold sweat started up on the back of her neck.

"I tied the cord around her neck, wrapped her in the bloody sheets, and stuffed her in the trash can." And her smile widened, as though Sister Agnes had done something incredibly clever.

So there it was. The last puzzle piece. Agnes

of God. Science had triumphed; welcome to the twentieth century.

A low, heartbroken moan escaped Mother Miriam Ruth. "No! Ah, no. She remembered. And all this time I thought she was some unconscious innocent. But she knew. She knew."

Martha Livingston's shoulders slumped in despair.

"One, two, three," she said quietly.

And Sister Agnes woke up.

Fifteen

Of course, Agnes didn't come to trial. How could she, disturbed as she was? Mother Miriam Ruth still said she was touched by God. Ironic. In the Middle Ages, crazy people carried with them an aura of reverence. They were called *simple*, and *natural*, and *touched by God*. They were sacred. The native Indian tribes of North America also considered their madmen to be sacred, somehow holy. So it seemed that Mother Miriam Ruth had been right all along. Sister Agnes *was* touched by God.

She was innocent; to that conclusion Dr. Martha Livingston had come at last. She didn't think the word *kill* was in Agnes's vocabulary. Agnes had been told so often that babies were a mistake, and Martha was sure she only wanted to correct a mistake, just as she said. A dying nun hallucinated and Agnes, a mystic who saw visions and received the stigmata, was sent to keep a rendez-vous with God. Nine months later, a mistake followed. How was Sister Paul to know? How was Sister Agnes to know?

All her life Martha had looked for answers. She always thought that if you asked the right questions, the right answers would be instantly forthcoming. She had never believed those who said that to some questions there were no an-swers. That was not the scientific way. What she felt was so beautiful about science was that it taught her the right questions to ask. But not all of them. For the first time she acknowledged that she didn't know all of them.

She knew now that there were some who turned to science, and some who turned to God, though in essence everybody looked for the same thing, the same answers to the same questions. Some experiment, some pray, and sometimes answers are forthcoming and sometimes they're not.

Martha found it somehow amusing that Mother Miriam Ruth and she were standing in each oth-er's shoes now. They'd made a half circle, the two of them, a full one hundred and eighty de-grees. The nun had believed in Agnes's inno-cence, now she didn't. The psychiatrist didn't and now she did. Amusing, but bitter. Martha had a dry taste in her mouth these days, like ashes, a taste she never had when she smoked.

They didn't bring her to trial, not after Dr. Livingston laid her report on Justice Leveau's desk. There was a hearing instead, at which Martha testified to the young nun's insanity. Mother Miriam Ruth, looking very tired and much older, came and gave her testimony, corroborative but brief. She mentioned the girl's visions but didn't dwell on them, and made no mention of the stigmata. There was a courtroom full of reporters at the hearing; better let well enough alone. None of the other nuns were questioned. Everybody was glad to get the business over with.

Throughout the hearing, Agnes sat as if carved from stone, unseeing and unhearing. She stared vacantly into space. On the way in, she had to pass through a barrage of newspaper cameras aimed in her direction and flashbulbs going off in her eyes. Only then did she flinch.

It wasn't a long hearing. Perhaps two hours, perhaps less. When the last witness had been called and had stepped down, Justice Leveau presented his decision.

"It seems quite clear that the defendant was in no manner responsible for her actions. It is therefore the judgment of this court that she be returned to the convent of Mary Magdalene, where she will be cared for under proper medical supervision by a visiting physician."

Sitting several rows behind Mother Miriam Ruth and Sister Marguerite, Martha Livingston could see the mother superior slump down in her seat with relief. The nun turned her head and looked directly at the psychiatrist, and Martha thought she had never seen such suffering in anyone's eyes before.

Having delivered the judgment in English, Justice Leveau was now prepared to render it again in French, as the law required. But just as he began, Sister Agnes rose to her feet.

There was a palpable hush in the courtroom as all eyes turned to the young nun. Everyone was waiting for her to speak, but she said . . . nothing.

"Oui?" asked Leveau encouragingly.

The girl seemed to want to speak, but it was as if she knew no words. Mother Miriam Ruth leaned forward in her chair, one hand out beseechingly, but Agnes did not look in her direction. Neither did she turn to Dr. Livingston. She just stood there.

"Do you have something to say?" the judge asked.

Agnes nodded. It was plain now that she was waiting for permission from Justice Leveau. He nodded back at her, granting it.

She didn't raise her voice, but spoke very quietly. Yet her voice was so clear that it carried to the back of the half-empty courtroom. Her words were simple, and her tone almost without expression.

"I stood in the window of my room every night for a week. And one night I heard the most beautiful voice imaginable, and when I looked, I saw the moon shining down on Him. For six nights He sang to me. Songs I've never heard. And on the seventh night He opened His wings and lay on top of me. And all the while He sang." And then, in the sweetest voice imaginable, the voice of a child's guardian angel, Sister Agnes began to sing. The song was more than two hundred and fifty years old, from a land far away.

Charlie's neat and Charlie's sweet,
And Charlie he's a dandy,
Every time he goes to town,
He gets his girl some candy. . . .

There was a shocked silence, then a rustle of talking in the courtroom. "Please remove her from the court," Leveau said quietly.

Sister Marguerite stood up and tried to pull the girl back into her seat, but Agnes continued to sing.

Over the river and through the trees,
Over the river to Charlie's,
Over the river and through the trees,
To bake a cake for Charlie. . . .

Now the judge was banging his gavel, and his voice rose sternly over the song. "Would someone please remove the defendant from the courtroom?" he demanded.

The sergeant-at-arms stepped forward and placed a restraining hand on the young nun's shoulder, but Mother Miriam Ruth shook her head no. She rose to her feet and, taking Agnes gently by the arm, led her quietly away. As they left the courtroom, the news photographers began snapping at her again, like barracudas with

cameras, their flashbulbs exploding in her pale
face. As she drew abreast of Dr. Livingston, Agnes looked at her without a word.

Once before they had looked into each other's
faces like this, strangers in the glare of the mer-
ciless flashbulbs. That first day on the courthouse steps, after the indictment. Surrounded by
all those nuns, and with her eyes so wide Martha
couldn't see what color they were. I didn't know
her then, Martha thought. But do I know her
now? And will I ever see her again?

Martha never expected to see any of them again,
but in the end she had to go back. In her long and
painful quest for the truth, many questions yet
remained unanswered, though she knew that there
were no answers for most of them. There were
no answers, really, for most of the important
matters of life. We ask "Why?" and God—or
Science—says "Because," and that's that. But
Martha wanted to ask Mother Miriam Ruth why
she had left Agnes alone to bear a baby in pain
by her terrified self.

"Agnes said she didn't want any help," she'd
said once, but that was no answer. No answer at
all.

And the man. Had Sister Paul really hallucinated and sent Agnes to him, as she'd told them
under hypnosis? In court Agnes said that she'd
seen a man from her window six nights running.
Was that the truth? Had she confided in Sister
Paul that she'd seen him in the barn? That God

Himself was in the hayloft? And had Sister Paul, at the end of her long life, made Agnes a present of the secret passage? If she did, was it because she, too, thought the man was God, or was it because she knew that he was not? Did she regret the long decades of her own celibacy and want something else for Agnes? Or were they two religious fanatics sharing a complex *folie à deux*? There were so many questions to which Martha would never know the answers. And she'd have to learn to live with that. But it was hard, damn it, it was hard!

"What are you doing here?" asked the mother superior.

"I had to come," Martha answered in a low voice. "How is she?"

In the weak afternoon sunlight of an unexpectedly glorious December day, Mother Miriam Ruth looked old and drained, as though the juice had been pressed out of her, leaving only the dry husk. Deep lines cut through her face, between her brows and at the sides of her nose and mouth.

Beyond her, in the stubbled fields, the Little Sisters walked in procession, chanting a blessing on the fields. It was a ceremony so ancient that it predated Christianity by several millennia. Martha had been watching it, standing alone in the sharp winter wind, when the nun had come up and addressed her.

"She doesn't talk to anyone anymore," said

Mother Miriam Ruth flatly. "And she's stopped singing altogether."

Martha's lips quivered, and a tear rolled down her cheek. "I'm sorry."

From a distance, the sound of the nuns' singing was carried to them on the wind, then carried off again as the wind shifted.

"I miss her," continued Martha, brushing the tears away.

But Mother Miriam Ruth didn't answer; nobody, she felt, could miss Agnes as much as she herself did, now that the girl had slipped away from her and was growing more distant and more feeble day by day.

"What did that song mean? The one she sang? Do you know?"

The nun shrugged. "Probably his song of seduction. Whoever *he* was."

"Maybe it was. But then couldn't it have been a lullabye . . . from her childhood . . . ?"

Mother Miriam Ruth shook her head. "And the father?"

Martha had no answer. "I don't know. Hope. Love. Desire."

"A belief in miracles," added the mother superior sadly.

Dr. Livingston sighed deeply. "I don't know what I believe anymore. But I want to believe," she told the reverend mother. "I want to believe that she was . . . blessed. . . ."

Mother Miriam Ruth's eyes opened wide in surprise. "Why?"

Now the tears were flowing full, down Martha's cheeks and onto the collar of her jacket. She made no attempt to stop them, because no power on earth or in heaven could have stopped them.

"Because . . . I . . . need her!" she sobbed.

Each of them took one step toward the other, and Mother Miriam Ruth, her eyes filling with her own tears, held her hand out to Martha Livingston. Because they understood what they shared. Each of them had been touched by Agnes of God, and each had taken something from her. A little piece of . . . faith . . . so that their lives were changed forever.

And, as they embraced, weeping, the wind brought another song to them. Or did they imagine it? Did they only think they heard Sister Agnes singing the *Agnus Dei*, pure as the winter air itself?

Agnus Dei, qui tollis peccata mundi,
Dona nobis pacem. . . .

Lamb of God, who taketh away the sins of the world, give us peace.

Amen.

More Biography and Autobiography from SIGNET

**Buy them at your local
bookstore or use coupon
on last page for ordering.**

World Renowned Authors from SIGNET

**Buy them at your local
bookstore or use coupon
on next page for ordering.**

Recommended Reading from SIGNET